HOW MAO DIED

A Chinese Love-story

DAVID E. R. GEORGE

How Mao Died: A Chinese Love-story
David E. R. George

FIRST PUBLISHED 2006 BY
SWALLOW TAIL PUBLISHING
MARGARET RIVER
WESTERN AUSTRALIA

ISBN 1-921019-56-5

TYPSET IN TIMES NEW ROMAN

DESIGNED BY: INK TANK: © BRUNO CHARPENTIER

CONVERSATIONS

Shanghai, 1928: The Bar of the Palace Hotel, International Settlement:
"The Reds? Been wiped out, buddy. A few bandits still, up in the hills..."
"Your Chinaman doesn't know how to fight..."
"I'll drink to that."
"What about this guy called Mao?"
"Dead."
"Assassinated."
"Sick with TB, I hear, or syphilis: you know they share their women around, don't you?"
"How do you know that? Have you ever been there? Has anyone ever been there?"
"Impossible, buddy. Can't be done..."

Peking, 1936: A quiet house near The Forbidden City:
"I got it! Look!"
He spills the contents of his bag on the floor: a dozen thick notebooks, thirty reels of film, a black jade snuff-box, Mao's cap, an elastic band...
"This is going to cause a sensation, Peg."
His face is thin, sporting a red, bristling beard; he begins to dance around the room:
"This changes everything..."

Washington, 1949 (or any time thereafter): The White House, The Oval Office:
The President (any President after 1949): "How did we lose China? I want heads, on plates... Who lost us China?"
"You want the long answer, or...?"
"Short."
"We should have listened to Ed Snow."

PART ONE

RED DAWN

"All this was a long time ago, I remember,
And I would do it again, but set down
This set down
This: were we led all that way for
Birth or Death? There was a Birth, certainly.
We had evidence and no doubt..."

T.S. Eliot,
Journey of the Magi

Euphoria.

I am cycling through the pink dawn across the open heart of Peking on my brand-new, shiny-black, one-gear, hard-saddle bike, brown paper wrapping flapping in the spokes like swaddling cloths.

The bike hadn't been hard to choose: there was only one model.

I am euphoric: I've got here.

I have jet-lag: I've been here less than twenty-four hours.

Unlike Ed Snow, this is not my first Asian country: I've done the exotic East. But here: no dead-eyed beggars plucking at your sleeve, no snarling traffic, open sewers or bright-painted child whores lurking outside the public toilets. I've lived in India, Malaysia, Thailand, Indonesia, but this is like no place I've ever been. Here I could be on the moon.

The cyclist in front of me is a woman, two little plaits lying black and shiny at the nape of her neck like a swallow's tail. The meticulously neat parting is like scar-tissue.

She cycles methodically, body hardly moving: I adjust my own enthusiastic pumping until I am in time with her, in time with a million whirling wheels. I want to reach out, call out to them all, but they are intent, serious, focused on the collective rhythm of whispering tyres and tinkling bells. There are so many of them and they are so close that if one of them misses the beat, there will be an accident.

They don't look like people engaged in one of the greatest experiments in human history, the radical transformation of human nature. But then there is nothing to compare them with: what would people look like after they'd learned to think and feel selflessly? The lines on your face are etched there by worry, fear, anger, sadness; what emotions would you have left after you learn how to live and work for everybody? You wouldn't need ambition; you wouldn't need anger or jealousy, spite, greed, lust...

I'm not sure about love...

I follow the woman with the swallow-tail plaits across the Square of Heavenly Peace. Peking is grey, blue, green, white, flashes of red. Grey the officials' uniforms, the tiles of the roofs, the hair of the leaders; green the military uniforms, leaves, hearts; blue the buses, bicycle license plates, waste bins; white the shirts, policemen's caps, teeth. Red the palace walls, armbands, bloodshot eyes... There is the great Gate into the Forbidden City, there the balcony where Mao stood and waved as a million Red Guards marched past, bathing in the euphoria of his Buddha-smile. Did they even notice the white man up there with him, the "long- nose;" do they know how much we all owe him for first canonizing their leader? For we are all Ed Snow's spiritual children.

Is it true that Mao is dying, mummified inside his own myth? Does it matter? They say there's going to be another Cultural Revolution any day now: it is seven years since the last one and he said there will be one every seven years until there's no need for leaders any more, no need for politics at all. In a country of good people, you don't need laws, and therefore no lawmakers: they can all pack up and join the workers, for we are all workers.

Last night, they gave a welcoming dinner for us in the echoing dining-hall, feeding us tidbits with their chopsticks - duck tongues, fish eyes - toasted us with fiery Mao-Tai in little porcelain cups:

"We are grateful Doctor David has come ten thousand miles to work with us."

"I am grateful you have let me come to learn from you, and please call me comrade - or just plain David if I haven't yet earned the title."

Back in the early Seventies, most of the world still declined to recognize the Peking regime as the legitimate government of China. To get here, to get to work in China, I had to go to London to be interviewed. There was a Chinese Embassy in London, which also has the best children's hospital in the world: my older daughter, Tracey, had been born with a hole in her heart and needed an operation, and my younger daughter Jessica had never met her grandparents.

All the signposts pointed in the right direction.

They'd told me to bring an autobiography. In it I stressed my class background: it had soured my youth but now it bears fruit:

"I was born to working class parents, my father a ticket collector on the Underground, my grandfather a navvy, my grandmother a charwoman. When the war ended and my father returned, he found my mother had run off with a Polish airman. He brought me up with very simple guidelines: work hard and you can become whatever you want to be; education is the key to success; whatever you want you must earn. Armed with these solid proletarian virtues (yes, I really did write that), I won scholarships to University where I studied foreign languages, was elected chairman of the United Nations Association, organized World Refugee Year, earned a Ph.D. at 23 and then got out. Hating the class system which had humiliated me, rejecting a system which educated bright working class children to become the servants or members of the bourgeoisie, I took a job in Berkeley, California..."

It was (but aren't they all?) a very selective autobiography (I didn't tell them about stealing the counting shells from kindergarten, breaking the windows at primary school, pissing in the neighbours' milk bottles... Or that my father told me that the one thing he'd learned from the war was "never join anything.")

Even then I wanted to be a writer and knew you have to meet the reader half way.

The autobiography worked because I'm here, have met some of my new colleagues: there are only thirty-seven of us in the whole of Peking - "long-noses," "round-eyes," who work for the Chinese government. We are all housed together in the Friendship Guesthouse along with Venezuelan rebels, Palestinian terrorists, African guerrilla leaders, but already I have plans to move out. We'll get our own place - like that one, a Chinese house with mud walls and a brick bed heated with millet stalks; we'll make beancurd in a big earthenware jar, Tracey will go to kindergarten with an abacus and a little red scarf; we'll catch crickets for Jessica in the rice fields and in the holidays we'll go to Yenan to see the cave where Mao lived, and follow the route of the Long March.

I notice that someone has a sidecar attached to their bike: we'll get one of those, for the children... The man with the sidecar looks up, sees me, is momentarily startled, his wheel snags another, the woman in front of me jerks desperately at the handlebars but too late: she falls off. Now I can see her face: the skin smooth over delicate bones, but she must be fifty at least. Momentarily the eyes registers shock, alarm, but then her face recovers, the muscles relax, smoothing the useless emotions away like the surface of a lake when the wind suddenly dies. I have stopped, placed one foot on the ground, poised to jump off and help. She looks at me; our eyes meet; hold; then she turns away, gathers her bike, gets back on and cycles away.

It was only a moment, but already I knew I wanted to write about this woman. I have so many questions: where were you in 1936, 1949, 1967; who chopped off your hair? I am here to ask questions, to see for myself. Back in Berkeley, California everyone had the answers already: revolution means saying fuck in public, planting vegetables in vacant lots and attending class without grades. They called themselves Trotskyists, Marcusian Marxists, Weathermen, but they were all the sons and daughters of accountants and interior decorators, for whom revolution is an excuse to bristle with self-righteousness and moral exhibitionism. They had a lot to be grateful for, had been given so much - everything, except the one thing that matters: something to use all that energy for, something to believe in. We'd gather in groups under the arthritic plane trees around the fountain and came to the same conclusion: whatever it was, it was somewhere else. India perhaps - gurus and ganja; Arizona - medicine-men and mescaline; Russia... I did all that, fueled by wanderlust and because I have to interrogate my dreams, see what they're like in the harsh light of day. Russia was the biggest disappointment, turned me off Communism completely: it seemed just an excuse to play the bully, institutionalize mediocrity, get your own back and feel smug at the same time. It didn't cure my hunger, or even suggest a suitable diet. But now they say there is this other version, a new covenant, the Chinese option.

I had to come and see for myself.

We have reached the entrance to a park and the woman stops, gets off her bike. An immense concrete screen blocks the gate to keep the ghosts out: it is swirling white on blood red - a poem by the Chairman, called "Snow." I recognize it immediately: he wrote it during the Long March, forty years ago. The concrete screen has cracked in the dry air, blobs of cement obscure parts of the poem, white dashes and dribs like bird-shit on a field of poppies. The woman doesn't even look at it, wheels her bike round the ghost-screen and then along a dusty canal to a bridge where she stops. Has she come to meet her lover? I have come to live a love-story and maybe write one too. I have this great yearning hunger, I want to write a book which will make people feel that life has joy in it and purpose, a book about the other happiness - not the one which feeds on personal success, vanity, recognition, but the happiness that comes from feeling part of a community, carrying out a great vision, losing oneself in it.

I have this cursed need to believe that California doesn't have all the answers, that there must be an alternative, and that I can find it.

Because when the world runs out of alternatives, it will stop turning, and we will all fall off.

I already have a name for the book: I'm going to call it "How The Swallow Lost Its Tail." I found it in the unpublished papers of the man, who, more than anyone else, has led me here. He owes me one - not because he lied, but because he, like all of us, sometimes let his visions get in the way of his eyes. But then memory does live next door to the imagination, doesn't it, and the wall is porous? The Chinese have never believed that there is one, single reality, which can be known as it is and not the way we see it. They had absorbed Buddhism before they ever heard of Marxism - which also has no special commitment to mere facts: "If the facts don't fit the theory," wrote Hegel, "then it is the facts which are wrong." It's easy to smile knowingly, dismiss that as dishonest, deceptive: "Sly little bastards, aren't they? Clever, but cunning." One day the Chinese will announce that they taking up Capitalism and everyone will smile and congratulate themselves, forgetting that - in Marx and in Lenin too - Capitalism is a necessary stage on the way to Communism. Where else can proletarian consciousness come from? If, in the not-too distant future, they then complete the Capitalist stage and go on to the next, offer the world a real option, it will be our fault if we're shocked. Those who don't learn from history are doomed to repeat it - wrote Marx. I am here because Mao has revised the theory, says there's another way, a Chinese way. In Chinese the word for knowledge - Tao - represents a man in a flowing robe and a head: to know is to walk through life, recording what you see. Don't ask if it's fact or not. Fact is only the past tense of fiction...

But I digress; I am lost. Just inside the park, an old man is writhing his way through his Tai Chi exercises, eyes on his ring-finger or, as they call it, "the finger that has no name." That's strange: I thought Tai Chi was banned now, along with goldfish, make-up, crickets in cages, gambling, long hair, narrow trousers, finger-guessing, American cigarettes, leather shoes, cats? In the shade of a stunted pine tree, a clump of men squat by their donkey-carts in dark, patched clothes, snapping down cards, soft and creased with handling. They have big teeth and cropped heads, deal the cards from right to left, snapping them down with delighted venom. What are they betting on? Dare I ask them the way; will anyone understand my Chinese - learned in Malaysia where I first read Mao's poems and then his speeches and we adopted Tracey. What will she make of all this? Last night, at the welcoming dinner, one of the comrades said:

"She doesn't look like you?"

"She's adopted. Chinese."

"Ah, we sold her to you."

"No," we smile. But they know that children are sold in the capitalist world:

"It used to be that way here too..."

Back in our room, Tracey sits down inside an empty suitcase on the floor of our bare, brown, narrow apartment, walls pock-marked with someone else's thumbtacks:

"Is this our new home?"

"Yes, poppy. For now..."

And with that directness of children, she looks up:

"Why?"

You could see she was disappointed and it was a bit dismal, but to answer her question then would have taken too long. And it is a puzzle, isn't it - when you try to trace your life backwards, pinpoint all the chance encounters, casual phrases, looks, each of which was somehow connected to other encounters, phrases, looks, accidents, until they made a chain, a net? I could start by giving her my autobiography, but to answer her question properly, I'd have to tell her about Cambridge, about Berkeley, California, about Jiang Qing, Fanshen...

Above all, I'd have to tell her about Ed Snow

I

He'd never seen anything like it.

Standing, shocked into temporary immobility, on the steps of the YMCA, Ed looked down at the street milling with half-naked coolies bowed under sagging bamboo poles, careening rickshaws, women in men's trousers and bobbed hair, hawkers dodging the thick sticks of turbaned Sikhs, missionaries with Bibles, and a man pushing a wheelbarrow loaded with gold and silver bars escorted only by a pompous clerk in a blue silk gown.

Ed couldn't even identify what half of them were doing. But then he had nothing to compare them with. This was Ed's first encounter with Asia - not counting the brief stopover in Japan where he'd arrived as a stowaway and had to leave in a hurry.

He who had wanted to be a news reporter, found that he was the story.

Japan was charming and orderly; Shanghai was like nothing he'd ever experienced in all his twenty-two years: it was all so unbelievably alive, the scene so vivid to his virginal eyes, he could still conjure it up in precise detail decades later: "a continuous freak circus with all manner of people performing almost every physical and social function in public, yelling, gesturing, always acting, crushing throngs spilling through every kind of traffic; coolies racing wildly to compete for ricksha fares, 'honey-carts' filled with excrement; perfumed, exquisitely gowned, mid-thigh-exposed Chinese ladies, singing peddlers bearing portable kitchens ready with delicious noodles on the spot, gambling mah-jongg ivories clicking and pari-mutuel betting, the endless hawking and spitting, the baby's urine stream on the curb..."

And this was only the Bund, the wide, flower-lined avenue along the Whangpoo River; this was not yet the Chinese city.

But Ed hadn't come all this way to stand in the no-man's land of a hotel steps: brushing his hands through his thick wavy hair, he walked down the steps and into the crowd. And, at first, it was all half-familiar after all: the towering gray stone pile of Jardine and Matheson's, the British Consulate, the Bank of Indochina, the Russo-Asian Bank, the Tudor Customs Building, monuments to Sir Harry-this and Sir Robert-that. The reassuring pyramid to the "Ever Victorious Army" of Western mercenaries who had suppressed the Taiping rebels - only sixty years ago. He crossed the Wu song, passed the Astor House Hotel and entered the International Concession. But then he stopped. This could be the Eastern Seaboard, he thought, or a French provincial town with its wide streets of stately homes and smug lawns behind walls topped with broken glass. The streets were all laid out in a regular, orderly checkerboard - like New York, except that the avenues running North-South were named after Chinese provinces - Hunan, Shanxi, Szechuan - and the streets running East-West bore the names of Chinese cities - Peking, Nanking...

A gang of American sailors strolled past, bragging about how many women they'd had: "ten, pal, all naked, dancing on the bed and then making love to each other in between filling my glass with bubbly." They glared at a group of Japanese sailors in blue jackets and long swords walking in the other direction: "Fucking Nips: they get my goat."

And so he turned and strolled back, sniffing his way along the Bund like a dog reassuring himself of his bearings. On the river, white ships floated at anchor, fan-sailed junks and gunboats, their cannon trained inwards on a China he couldn't even guess at yet. On he went, through the French Concession with its Russian restaurants where pale women sat, dressed in furs, sipping lemon tea and playing patience, then through a gate in the ramparts and he was suddenly in another world. A man in a long gray robe and a pigtail plucked at his sleeve: "You want guide? Not safe without guide. I show you good time."

Ed shrugged him politely off;

"You want opium? Sing-song girl, golden boy...?" the man called after him as he plunged into the labyrinth of narrow streets not wide enough to take a car. The smells almost knocked him over but he'd come for an adventure, hadn't he? People kept holding things out to him - baroque goldfish in bowls, crickets in cages, leather shoes, cats, cans of American cigarettes... A gang of boys in school uniforms jostled him: they were chasing a barefooted child in ragged clothes, calling out names at him and jeering. They cornered him outside a cinema and began to pelt him with sticks and stones. The boy crouched at bay, snarling, then picked up the stones and threw them back, crying out in venomous joy when he struck one of his tormenters on the forehead, making it bleed. Ed felt someone push a leaflet in his hand, but when he looked round, the messenger had melted back into the crowd; anxiously he checked his back pocket and then removed his wallet and placed it inside his jacket. He must get some new clothes: Shanghai was hot and sticky, not a place to be wearing a tweed jacket, plus-fours and ribbed knee socks.

Suddenly a small lake beckoned, in the middle a teahouse joined by a zig-zag bridge; he thought of taking temporary relief there, but the tables were all occupied by young people, talking earnestly through clouds of cigarette smoke while others sat hunched over gaudy movie magazines with pictures on the cover of Mae West and Clark Gable.

He moved on, through a park with a stream and a little curved red bridge where a woman stood gazing wistfully down, past a temple guarded by fierce, red-faced statues: he was lost, didn't dare trust his few words of Chinese, struggled on and managed to hail a silver-colored Morris taxi which deposited him safely back on the steps of the YMCA.

Whew!

Ed had letters of introduction: he already knew the value of personal connections, and the next day presented himself at the offices of J.B. Powell on the sixth floor of the Great Northern Telegraphy Building on the Avenue Edward VII. Wavy hair brushed back from his broad, domed forehead, he was dapper in knitted tie and pocket handkerchief. He handed Powell the letter from the

Dean of Journalism at the University of Missouri, his Alma Mater and Powell's own home state.

J.B. took it, read it, tapped out his corncob pipe, looked up from his cluttered desk; Ed had been admiring the books lining his walls:

"Well, Mr. Snow, now tell me in your own words: what are you doing here?"

Ed gave the answer he always gave back then, the one he'd given his father when he eventually dared write to him - from Hawaii, already safely halfway across:

"I plan a year of traveling around the world. Then I'll return to New York, make a fortune before I'm thirty, and devote the rest of my life to leisurely study and writing."

It really did look that easy in 1928.

He planned, he said, to finance it by writing travel pieces freelance.

He didn't know then that, in fact, he'd remain here, in China, for the next thirteen years. If you'd told him that then, he'd have laughed that boyish laugh of his:

"I've allotted six weeks to China. Then I'm off to India, Russia..."

If you'd told him then that he'd bring off one of the greatest scoops in journalistic history, he'd have smiled more seriously, nodded:

"Yes, well, I'd like to be a crackerjack reporter. But a scoop? What's the story?"

Later, when Ed had done all these things, he'd sometimes look back and wonder what network of chance encounters, overheard phrases, casual looks had woven his life for him:

"When I first reached Shanghai I was every youth, full of curiosity and wide open to the world. I could have been anyone of my generation."

Yes, but what makes a man different, Ed? What are the signposts on the road to his distinction from others? Ed traced one line back to his genes: "I was moved," he said, "like my forebears, by the pull of some frontier dream, some nameless beckoning freedom."

Missouri had bred in him its spirit of pioneering adventure, of self-reliance and personal enterprise: 'Show Me,' said Missouri. But it was also a racist culture: Ed's father hated cities because, he said, they were dominated by Jews, Spics, Bolshies and other foreigners. In Shanghai, at first, Ed himself still referred to the Chinese as "slant-eyes." He'd only known one Chinese in Kansas City: he owned the laundry near the grocery store and Ed and the other kids would creep up and yell a ditty they'd learned from Crazy Mary, their Negro washerwoman, who resented the foreign competitor:

"Chinaman, Chinaman, eat dead rats!

Chew them up like gingersnaps."

It used to make the Chinaman come running out, pigtail swinging, and curse them back - until he found the better tactic was just to ignore them, so they lost interest in baiting him.

But none of that explained how a boy from Kansas City now found himself in Shanghai - except that if you roam far enough West, you're bound to end in the Far East. Missouri had given him a lot to be grateful for - all except one thing: something to believe in. Ed's Mum had tried: she was a Papist with priests on both sides of the family; his Dad had agreed to study Catholic doctrine - just enough to marry the beautiful redhead. But he refused to send Ed to parochial school and delighted in eating meat on Fridays while everyone else ate fish. Ed lost his faith when he went with another altar-boy to collect the host and was shocked to find that the communion wafers were baked in an ordinary coal oven. On the way back, he opened one of the tins and consumed, on the spot, the body of Christ. He waited under the flat, empty, prairie sky, but nothing happened: no sudden illumination, no bolt from heaven either. It left a hole in his soul, which he somehow expected to fill one day with some other revelation.

He didn't expect it to be political, though he was already a bit of a rebel, running away from home when he was fourteen - to California, riding the freight trains until robbed of his last fifty cents by migrant farm-workers. But he saw the Pacific and dreamed of one day sailing across it. When he got back, he found his father less domineering, more tolerant. It confirmed in him what he'd learned from the Irish settlers on his mother's side: "Morality," they said, "is always on the side of the rebel."

Some of this he told J.B. that hot, sticky morning in Shanghai, and Powell did ask him about journalism.

"Well," said Ed, "I guess I breathed that in with the air. My Dad had a print shop where I worked for my pocket-money: I loved the smell of the ink, the fresh-cut paper... I started a fraternity newspaper at high school and studied journalism at University. I worked for an ad agency in New York," he added: "good publicity is essential if you want to sell your ideas, don't you think?"

"Hm," said J.B., and then: "Do you want a job?"

"As a reporter?"

"Kind of. It just so happens I'm looking for someone to do a little job for me. A special for The China Weekly Review. I'm calling it "New China." I want to focus on the way they're rebuilding the railways, the telegraph system. I want it to be upbeat, optimistic, positive - it could suit you. We need to persuade Americans that now the Reds are suppressed, it's safe to travel in China again. Asia's changing, Mr. Snow, and we have to change with it. It used to fuel our dreams of the exotic, our wet-dreams of sensuality, luxury and decadence, a source of cheap labor and a huge market for our goods. But Chiang Kai-shek is changing things. He's the big hope for China - the only one who'll stand up to the Japs. They're the real enemy, my friend, not the Reds. China's enemy, and ours too. We've got to make China a friend, an ally, start treating her as an equal. Hell, we Americans are supposed to side with the underdog, aren't we?"

Ed nodded, still not convinced.

"You did say you wanted to write travel pieces," J.B. pressed him: "This will give you a chance to see the rest of the country. You can travel the whole length of the railroad - it's OK, you'll have a private V.I.P. carriage - and I'll give you C.T. Washington Wu to smooth the way for you. What do you think?"

"Well, thank you, Mr. Powell, that sure is a very generous offer, but I've allotted only six weeks to China, and…"

"Stay for six weeks. Then leave if you still want to. My guess is you'll like it and stay."

"But…I know nothing about China…"

"Exactly: you won't think you have all the answers. Just tell the facts as you see them. Is it a deal?"

Ed hesitated, then put out his hand.

"Good," said J.B. "you start tomorrow. Oh, and get yourself a change of clothes. Linen's best… Come on, I'll take you to my tailor."

And as Ed walked the streets of Shanghai for only the second time, J.B. gave him a few pointers:

"Just forget everything you think you already know. Here they read from right to left, put surnames first and given names last, wave you away when they wish to beckon, put their hands in their sleeves instead of shaking yours to say goodbye, pare an apple away from them instead of toward them, pull to saw a piece of wood instead of pushing, deal cards from left to right, drink soup at the end of the meal and say 'no' when they mean yes… Here we are…"

And so Ed had himself measured for his first tailor-made suit.

They walked back to the office - J.B. wouldn't take a rickshaw: "One man shouldn't ride on the back of another man." They parted at the crossroads just outside the Chinese part of the city. A crowd had gathered around a group of twenty or so young girls and boys guarded by three men in Kuomintang uniforms. They were apparently being offered for sale and as Ed watched appalled, one potential buyer lifted the gown of a young girl.

"Famine refugees," said J.B.: "Or orphans of people killed by the Reds. Maybe neither, maybe they've been kidnapped. They're being sold as servants, or to brothels, the theatre - same thing. Yes, I know it looks bad but be careful not to judge what you don't yet know, otherwise you'll end up like everyone else, despising the lot of them. Out there," he gestured vaguely West: "there are villages inhabited only by piles of bones. You'll see."

He took out his fob-watch: "I got to go. I'll see you in the morning."

It was a pensive Ed who walked back to the YMCA, avoiding the eyes of the beggars squatting in the shade with their bare, crippled feet, black and rotting with gangrene, but unable not to stare in horror at the severed heads hanging, drying, on a lamppost under a stop sign, last spasm of the Kuomintang massacre of the Shanghai Communists.

Only one sight made him pause: a young girl - about ten, twelve - had been stopped by two plainclothes policemen and was being questioned. They were pointing at her hair which Ed noticed she wore short, and then at her feet which had not been bound. They kept thrusting a leaflet in her face accusingly. He couldn't understand what they were saying but he heard a word then he would soon learn, and use, and make famous: "Kungch'antang." They hurled it at her as a question, then an accusation, then an insult: "Kungch'antang?" "Kungch'antang!" It was a word Ed was soon to learn the meaning of: "Share-Wealth Party" - the Chinese name for Communist Party. The girl shook her head, looked round desperately for a way to escape, but the two men grabbed her by the arms and dragged her away. She looked back over her shoulder, eyes wide: they met Ed's; held the contact. It was only a moment, a look. He hardly thought about her for the rest of the day, but that night - the glance had been so intense - he saw her face again, now lodged in the cave of his memory. And his dreams.

Mr. Twenty-eight Strokes

That same year, at about the same time, some five hundred miles to the South-west, in the province of Hunan, not far from the capital, Changsha, a young man was hiding in the tall reeds round a pond.

He is on the run.

He has just heard that most of his friends in Shanghai are dead, their heads displayed on lampposts and in bamboo cages, the boys burned alive doused in kerosene or bound to trees and put to death by a thousand cuts into which salt and sand were rubbed; the girls killed by bullets fired up their vagina. Cautiously, the young man raises his head, careful that his glossy, long, black hair does not give him away. A posse of Kuomintang soldiers, aided by some peasants they have forced help them search, is beating the rice, making the crickets fly up, screeching in indignation and alarm. The young man slowly ducks his head back down: funny, he thinks with a wry smile, that it should have been by a pond such as this that he first raised the flag of rebellion against despotic power. His father had given a party to celebrate a successful business deal, had accused the boy of being lazy, lacking filial piety but the boy had cursed him and run away, taken up a defensive position on the other side of their duck pond. His father had pursued him, furious at the loss of face in front of his guests, demanded that the boy kow-tow, knock his head nine times on the ground in contrition. The boy shook his head defiantly:

"I'd rather jump in the pond and drown," he yelled. "Come a step closer and I will!"

The father hesitated: he had spent money on this boy, hard-earned cash, sent him to school to learn the abacus and the classics so he could keep the family accounts. Himself a poor peasant, he had managed by careful saving to buy land and now employed other peasants, rising by the only means he knew: selling his surplus, accumulating capital, speculating on prices, lending money at high interest rates - and all for this ungrateful boy, for the only social group he recognized and believed in: the family. It was all the fault of his damned wife, with her soft ways - giving away rice when the harvest was bad and taking the boy to worship at the Buddhist temple on Phoenix Hill. He had no time for her faith, no time for rebels either: it is not the Chinese way.

But he didn't want the boy to drown and knew that he was stubborn enough to do it. When the boy called back that he would compromise, agree to place one knee on the ground if his father promised not to beat him, he nodded.

As the young man would say later: "I learned then that if you defend your rights by open rebellion, the ruling power will relent, whereas if you remain meek and submissive, he will only curse and beat you the more."

But knowing what to rebel against is not the same as knowing what to rebel for: not Buddhism, he silently lectures the golden carp who hover open-mouthed by the lotus leaves wondering what he has to feed them. Temples should be turned into schools; it is education that China needs. After contemplating police school, law school, commerce school, even a soap-making institute, it was a teacher and a journalist the boy had decided to become.

So why had the Kuomintang picked him up, taken him to headquarters where he was to be shot? At first, he'd attempted to bribe the escort to free him, borrowing money from a comrade: the poor soldiers had been ready to take the money and let him go, but their subaltern refused. He had no option then but to run: two hundred yards from headquarters, he'd broken loose and taken to the fields, bullets whistling round his ears. Many times already they have come close to the pond, once or twice so close he could have reached out and touched them. If he can make it to dusk, he stands a chance. He knows the countryside around here like the mole on his chin. How many times he has tramped through it, bathing in the cold rain, sleeping in the open when the frost fell, swimming in icy rivers - always against the current. He already knew then that he was training himself for something, but didn't yet know what it was.

He feels no fear as a water snake pokes its head out of the slimy water, eying a praying mantis, and frogs hop out of the pond and look at him, inquiringly. All he feels is a quiet pride that he is imitating his heroes, the Robin Hood rebels of "The Water Margin" which he'd read surreptitiously at night, by a tiny oil-lamp, the window blacked out so his father couldn't see. Only one thing he'd missed in those classic romances: the heroes were all warriors, officials, scholars, never a peasant. Why? He soon found out: when the peasants in his area did rebel after a severe famine, they were arrested and beheaded, their heads displayed on poles in the street as a warning. But there had to be an answer somewhere and he knew only one place to find it - in books, where he first read about Washington and Lincoln and the American Revolution, and even more so in newspapers which he first discovered in Changsha when his father allowed him to go on to high school. He became a newspaper addict and, inspired by the power of the word, began to write himself, posting his first article on the school wall. It was against the foreign capitalists and made him, who had first been scorned for his ragged clothes, a hero among his schoolmates - especially after he led them to a protest meeting in town and showed them how to fill soft melons with dog shit and hurl them at the pompous official urging them to go home. It was then he cut off his pigtail - a symbolic act of defiance of the Manchus who ruled China. When some of his schoolmates failed to keep their word and do the same, he cornered them in a back alley and cut their pigtails off for them.

But that was not why they hunted him now through the rice fields of Hunan: no, he growls at the mosquitoes buzzing in his ears and the back of his neck, it is because he has found and now urges on others a new faith, a new belief. He knows precisely when it had happened, his moment of revelation. He had gone up to Peking, got a job as a library assistant so as to have free access to his beloved books, joined the Journalism Society and became involved in radical student politics, editing their newspaper. Poor, he rented part of the crumbling Fuyu lamasery on North Avenue near the moat of the Imperial Palace, sleeping in the main hall of the temple under the eyes of red-faced Buddhist guardian deities, his desk the incense table, next to it a mimeograph machine, the only property of what he proudly called The Common People's Cause News Agency. It was there, at that incense table in the lama temple, that he read the Communist Manifesto and first saw the name which was to become so sacred to him: Ma Ke-se, the German Marx - who also loved libraries.

But he didn't stay in Peking, finding it too cold and dusty for his Southern tastes, mocked for his provincial accent and straw sandals.

He went to Shanghai - to help found a new Party, holding sessions at first behind the black lacquer doors of a gray and pink villa on a street called prophetically Joyful Undertaking. They sat on wooden stools at a table cluttered with teacups and papers, the young man in a long gown which made him look like a Taoist priest:

"There is a theory," he argued: "it is the arrow, but some comrades simple fondle the arrow and say 'excellent arrow, excellent arrow.' It has no mystical value; it is simply useful. Everything else is dog shit."

When the Russian envoy Borodin bridled at this, the young man said laconically:

"Dog shit fertilizes the fields; man's shit feeds the dogs. But dogma - that can't fertilize fields or even feed the dog."

When they realized that the plainclothes police were on their trail, they resumed their sessions on a hired tourist boat on South Lake. It was there they decided on a name for their new party: Kungch'antang.

\ They were twelve, he tells the mantis, picking it up gently by the back of its neck and putting it safe in his pocket, showing his teeth to the disappointed snake. At first, they were in alliance with the Kuomintang, but in April 1927, Chiang Kai-shek converted to Christianity so as to marry a Methodist girl educated in America, and celebrated it by riding into Shanghai on a gunboat and sending in his Blue Shirts to massacre his erstwhile allies. Borodin packed his bags and left for Russia announcing: "It's all over."

The young man fled, tried to organize an uprising in Hunan but it was too early and too late. Now he is watching the lotuses on the pond, waiting for them to close as night comes on.

And then? As he has crouched there, waiting, the answers have come. He'll go back where he belongs: "China can be conquered only when every Hunanese is dead," says Hunan, and he isn't ready to die: he's going to live for two hundred years. He'll go away from the cities, back to the mud houses with their rice-stalk thatch roofs, red peppers dangling from the eaves, back to the yellow earth, the bamboo thickets and hills, back to the peasants. It was hardly classic Marxism, but what did Marx know about China, what did any of them know about China?

Well, they will soon know about him, he determines grimly, getting up, stretching his aching body and fading into the dark scrub.

He is barefoot, they had taken away his shoes - as booty and because a man who dies with his shoes on will return as a ghost and pursue his executioner in revenge.

Sometimes he calls himself Mr. Twenty-eight Strokes, because it takes twenty-eight brush strokes to write his name: Mao - meaning 'Hair' - Zedong, meaning 'Anoints the East.'

Our things have arrived - in two big packing cases. I wonder why we bothered. Things which seemed important back there have no relevance here: designer jeans, flower vases, insurance policies... We unpack the books and line our shelves with records - The Yes, Jefferson Airplane, Led Zeppelin. Who knows: sometimes we may feel nostalgic, though I doubt it. I have a contract to teach for two years at the Peking Institute of Broadcasting. One-way plane tickets. At the time I didn't question this: who knows, we may decide never to leave.

We have new friends: Fausto, a Columbian guerrilla with whom I do Tai Chi at dawn every morning out in the scruffy garden of crackling maize. Once the head of a University department and T.V. producer, he discovered he had a nagging conscience, formed an underground movement, was betrayed, escaped to the maquis where he blew up police posts and put on propaganda plays until they tracked him down and he had to flee the country.

He says he misses his wife and children but otherwise has no regrets.

Also Khaleel, a Palestinian headmaster who is here to study Mao's guerilla tactics and serves us coffee spiced with cardamom seeds and anti-Zionist rhetoric; Zoran, a Yugoslav in an American baseball cap; Karl, a Viennese bookseller with a beard and a wife with a mouth like a guillotine, and Ken, a lapsed Trappist monk who lives in the flat above ours where he plays Götterdämmerung very loud on an old wind-up gramophone. He spreads himself over one of the brown, dust-covered armchairs in our narrow apartment, pours the good beer and the bad brandy into his moon face and yells insults at the bug set up high in the wall, pretending to be a smoke detector, for this hotel had originally been built by the Chinese for the Russians.

We all work for a University or a publishing house; some have been here for years, used to live "out there" but now everyone has been moved into the Friendship Guesthouse - for security reasons, they say, though Ken says it's so we don't see what's really going on. He talks wistfully about getting permission to move out again, one day, but there are no advertisements for houses to rent in the newspapers. There are no advertisements.

Meanwhile, they come and sit at our table in the dining-room and tell us how to succeed with the Chinese:

"Never push them into a situation where they'll lose face: then they can't give in;"

"Always push them into a situation where they'll lose face: then they have to give in;"

"No, no, you don't understand: the really exquisite part of all this is that whoever takes away someone else's face, loses their face too..."

"Let them look after their faces; I'll look after mine;"

"Nah: the Chinese don't think we have faces."

And these are all Friends of China - or so it says on the little red badge we've all been given to wear on our lapel so that the Chinese we meet won't think we're spies.

What happened? Why is everyone so cynical?

"They asked too many questions," says Ken.

"But..."

"And they kept saying but..."

I don't listen: I am here because there's supposed to be a new kind of revolution going on and as Mao wrote: "If you want to know the taste of a pear, you must eat it yourself."

They have given me a new name, a Chinese name: Da Wei. It means the "Great Protector" and I have not come here to walk into someone else's house and immediately begin criticizing the furniture. So I go out on my bike, a white corpuscle among the red. It helps me to stop thinking, turn off the knitting machine which has stitched furrows in my brow, lose myself in the turning wheels under the blue sky, live for now for my beliefs and hopes. Later the mind can pick them over.

In the Square of Heavenly Peace, groups wait in patient lines for photographers with three-legged cameras to pose them in heroic tableaux against the backdrop of the Forbidden City. Am I too late? Mao lives behind those walls: is it true that he's dying? My daughter, Tracey, has become fascinated by him, his statue everywhere, made of rough white concrete:

"I'd like to eat Chairman Mao."

"Sh."

"But he looks like icing sugar."

Nobody seems to read the quotations from his works written in white characters on huge red screens at every crossroads, but perhaps they know them off by heart or, as the Chinese say: "on the back."

Every day a car collects me and drives me out to the Institute of Broadcasting. Just inside the entrance is a weed-worn garden around a huge concrete pedestal with no statue. There was once a statute, but it was knocked down during the Cultural Revolution, when the flowers were all pulled up too. The weeds are not telling why. On the walls of the grimy buildings, faded scraps of pink and green flimsy paper cling precariously, remnants of wall posters, now torn by the wind and run by the rain. They give me an office with a simple wooden desk; a carpenter comes and puts a lock on the drawer - which embarrasses me until I notice that everyone locks up their notebooks when they leave the room. I share the office with a Chinese teacher: Dong Ming - the name he assumed during the Cultural Revolution. It means "The East is Bright." He is a solid young man with a squarish head and a box-like mouth. I can barely understand a word he says when he speaks to me in English: he has completed his course in two years instead of four, has no diploma, sat no examination:

"They encourage bourgeois competitiveness."

He shows me the canteen, where he congratulates the food on being so cheap and wholesome; the common room where they all take an afternoon nap. I say that's not my habit but he assures me: "It is healthy to take forty blinks."

The job they have given me is to teach Chinese teachers of English how to teach it. It's not easy: Chinese has no articles. In

Chinese, you can't distinguish between "the man," "a man," and just "man." Russian's the same, whereas all the other languages I know enable us to distinguish individual, specific things - and people - from the whole. What will they do when they discover how we organize our thoughts, our world?

I set them essays every week, but they paste them together with sentences lifted wholesale from The People's Daily in which harvests are always "bumper," production quotas always "overfulfilled" and the leadership "at all levels". I try to explain to them what a cliché is, but they look scornful and say: why can't a true statement be repeated in the same way if it's true? When I tell them to beware of overusing heroic adjectives whereby the masses are always "bravely" fighting revisionism and the children all "boldly" studying MaoZedong-Thought, they say:

"What's the problem, can't people in the West be heroic any more?"

"It makes you sound too self-righteous," I say: "as if you've just invented heroism and morality."

They smile.

I ask them each to write an autobiography.

The suggestion clearly worries them: autobiographies are too much like the lengthy self-criticisms everyone had to write seven years ago.

So I give them mine as an example, tell them how I became a rebel, first as a child, refusing to sing solos in the Church choir until I got paid the same as the grown-ups and, when they refused, stealing a handful of Communion wafers, kneeling by my bed, placing them on my tongue, dismayed when all they did was melt. Then, when my Dad came back from the War with a new, Italian wife, she encouraged me to go out and steal fruit, though we didn't call that stealing, we called it scrumping and thought of it as a dare not a crime. It really shook me when I took some scrumped strawberries to Boy Scouts, sharing them around like a trophy, proof of my sense of initiative and courage, only to be soundly berated by the Scout Master who tore my badges from my shoulder. I left the

Scouts then, graduated to the Campaign for Nuclear Disarmament. But it was never really political, any of this: it was personal, a way of demanding attention, standing out from the rest, asserting my difference.

It was Berkeley and the Sixties which made me political, where I first read Mao and Snow.

I tell my class about Snow, amazed they have never heard of him. Perhaps they should read this book too?

II

Ed moved out of the YMCA and took a small apartment on Seymour Street with John Allison - who would one day be US Ambassador to Japan but was then a clerk in the Consulate, earning the same as Ed, 600 Chinese dollars a month. It wasn't much, but the rent was negligible and there was enough left over to keep up the front of a white man. Foreigners paid no taxes, and were not subject to Chinese law.

At first Ed just soaked it all in, going to the races, trying all the restaurants, eying the White Russian "widows" along Avenue Joffre, and the "Buddha of the future" in Long Hua Temple. The girl slipped down into the storehouse of his memory, her file labeled temporarily inactive. He bought tickets on the fourth floor of Sincere's Department Store where for one Yuan he could get three dances with a slender, bejeweled taxi-girl. He tried opium, but it made his skin itch unbearably and his stomach throw up in the gutter outside.

The six weeks of his original timetable stretched to three months - the time it took him to fill the two hundred pages of J.B.'s special on "New China" with copy and advertising. The three months ballooned out to a vague "year or so" when J.B., pleased with the young man's energy and fresh eye, promoted him to assistant editor. He got on well with J.B., cramming from his library, cribbing shamelessly to fill in what he didn't yet know. They had only one disagreement: The Review, like newspapers everywhere, depended on advertising revenue, but J.B.'s resolute anti-British, anti-Imperialism, pro-Chiang line irritated many potential clients. They called him "too radical," "a traitor to his class and color" and - the greatest sin of all: "pro-Chinese." Ed respected his experience and his staunch liberal stand, but felt you had to draw a line when your idealism gets in the way of commercial considerations.

J.B. sent him off to do a series of supplements on the tourist attractions along the Chinese railroad, and Ed did the grand tour, all 8,000 miles of it - in a private VIP carriage. He wrote articles for the Chinese Tourist Bureau about the mulberry trees and silk weavers around Lake Taihu, the temples and pagodas of Hangchow, the canals of Soochow, the Ming walls of Nanking, the sacred mountain of Tai Shan and the golden roofs and marble altars of Peking. He had himself photographed next to the image of Marco Polo in Yangchow, and was mistakenly reported captured by the Japanese on a trip to Jenan, which made him news again - for a few days. He loved his Chinese name which translated as "White Cloud;" he was falling in love - with a history that stretched back over three thousand years, and with his own freedom from routine, his license to wander and look and write about what he saw and be paid for it. He was especially proud of one article. The Review opposed social discrimination against the Chinese and had already succeeded in ending the exclusion policy in the clubs, parks and Bund gardens, but some office buildings still required Chinese to use separate entrances - such as the Cable Building itself where The Review was located. One day Ed was present when a Chinese official was denied passage in the front elevator, and wrote a satir- ical editorial about it, ridiculing the "Colonel Blimps of the Superior Race." It shamed the British owners of the building into changing their elevator policy, but when The Review's lease expired, J.B. was refused renewal and had to move offices.

Not that Ed especially liked the Chinese as a people - at least not those he met, and he was discovering that the easier they were to meet, the less he liked them. This was especially true of C.T. Washington Wu who been attached to him as a "technical expert," though his only claims to the position were some family connec- tions and that he was a returned student from America. Ed despised him for his ignorance about China, his fawning head-scraping to any higher official and sharp-tongued rudeness to his menials, not to mention his distasteful habit of sending for a girl every evening as an hors d'oeuvre before the sharks' fin soup.

As the six weeks stretched towards a full year, Ed started to feel

33

jaded. He'd got used to the bodies floating in the canals and the acrid stench of the honey-carts collecting night soil, was no longer aroused by the slit-skirt cheongsams or amused by the loud-mouthed, gaudy whores outside the 'flower-houses' along Bubbling Well Road, no longer disturbed by the pathetic corpses of little factory girls put out each morning with the other garbage. He found himself complaining about the endless bargaining that had to precede every rickshaw ride - "why can't they just set a fixed price?" -, the endless offers of plump ripe virgins - "who are about as virginal as a queen bee" -, the whining of the beggars with their naked, unwashed infants - "why don't they give them a good scrub?"

He began to ask just what he was doing here after all. It was no longer exotic, no longer glamorous, its only seduction the bind that there was nowhere else he could live in such luxury on such a wage.

All that changed in the late summer of 1929 when he went up to Saratsi to report on the famine in the Northwest.

It was a turning-point in his life, what he later called his "moment of awakening."

Saratsi was the end of the line, and as he stood there surveying the thousands who had crawled in from the blasted plains, he felt totally inadequate. Incongruous in white linen jacket and long white knee socks, he wandered through a landscape vomited up from Hell:

I need a movie camera for this, he thought, panning the scene: a crane shot, slowly drawing back and up to reveal an endless vista of suffering and dying. Ed noted the detail, the tight shots that tell: "In one place I saw a naked twig-armed child, his belly a balloon from a diet of leaves and sawdust. He was trying to shake back to life his naked father who had just died on the road." He came across a couple of young women: "their withered breasts hanging like deflated paper sacks, the color of the dried baked ducks dangling before a Chinese meat shop."

Not that there were any meat shops, the only meat that of human flesh stripped from corpses and offered for sale in the village streets.

The article he wrote on the famine was, by any standard, a great piece of reporting:

"Have you ever seen a man - a good honest man who has worked hard, a 'law-abiding citizen,' doing no serious harm to anyone - when he has had no food for more than a month? It is a most agonizing sight. His dying flesh hangs from him in wrinkled folds; you can clearly see every bone in his body; his eyes stare out unseeing. If he has been lucky he has long ago sold his wife and daughters. He has sold everything he owns, sometimes even the last rag of decency, and he sways there in the scorching sun, his testicles dangling from him like withered olive seeds - the last grim jest to remind you that this was once a man."

The dead were being heaped up in mounds outside the walls, waiting to be buried in shallow trenches - except that it was impossible to find enough men physically able to do the digging. The only healthy men were the money-lenders and their private police, traveling around, foreclosing on mortgages, taking over the land for a fraction of its normal value: a sack of grain could buy a whole farm. "A flood of vultures," he called them.

The children affected him most. He wrote about "their eyes, in which lingered no trace of the alert curiosity so characteristic of Chinese children, their little skeletons bent over and misshapen, their crooked bones, their little arms like twigs, and their purpling bellies, filled with bark and sawdust, protruding like tumors."

And he wrote about his anger: "These were not the most shocking things. The most shocking thing was that in many of those towns there were still rich men, rice hoarders and landlords, with armed guards to defend them. The shocking thing was that in the cities - where officials danced or played with sing-song girls - there were grain and food, and had been for months; that in Peking and elsewhere were thousands of tons of wheat and millet, collected by the Famine Commission, but which could not be shipped to the starving. Why not?"

His question hung unanswered in the still, fetid air; no-one was helping anyone - except for an American engineer brought in by the landlords to dig a new canal across the land they had just purchased for a song, and a medical missionary whose job was to keep the labor gangs deloused to prevent them catching the rampant typhus and plague. They - and a handful of Chinese helpers - carried a few emaciated victims back to the soup kitchens which the Salvation Army had rigged up in the town but "so many thousands were doomed, the salvation of a few lives seemed meaningless."

If only the keys of his old Corona typewriter could open doors, open eyes. Is the best I can do agonize over the choicest adjective?

He was standing, looking down at an old woman who was holding out a tiny body to him, skin tight against the cheekbones, eyes like black caves, stick limbs protruding from a swollen belly like needles from a ball of wool. Perhaps she wasn't so old, her skin slack and wrinkled, lips cracked, desiccated, eyes pools of pain, horrified by what they'd seen, lit only by a single thin dagger of pleading.

Ed had barriers he put up when this kind of thing happened: a journalist must remain objective, not get emotionally involved. It was the number one rule they had taught him at University; the very basis, they said, of journalistic ethics.

He did look around to see if there was anything he could give her to drink or eat. A girl - a teenager - was walking towards him. She belonged to a group of dozen or so young Chinese he'd noticed. By their clothes and accents they were from the South - or the South-West: Ed wasn't yet that good at those kinds of details. She was carrying a battered teapot in one hand and a basket in the other. She passed Ed, not even looking at him, knelt down in the dust by the woman, cradled her head and lifted the teapot to her lips, careful not to waste a drop. Then she picked up the baby and slowly, drop by drop, dribbled water on its lips which were glued together by parched saliva, until it opened a gaping, bottomless mouth.

"Yes, but: how do you choose?" Ed wanted to know but did not ask: "how can you choose to save one and condemn another - when you can't help them all?"

He must remember to put that in his article, the paralysis of impossible choice...

The girl passed the baby to its mother, opened the basket, and handed the woman an apple.

She took it in both hands, turning it, wonderingly.

The girl - the teenager - turned her head and looked up at Ed. Just enough to make him blush...

Then she stood up and walked on.

Five million people died that summer: it remained the most shocking experience of Ed's life - until he witnessed the furnaces and gas chambers of the Nazis: "who were too impatient to wait for mere starvation."

He filed his article - unhappily, doubting his ability, doubting his profession:

"Why don't they revolt?" he hammered the old typewriter: "Why don't they march in a great army and attack the scoundrels who can tax them but cannot feed them, who can seize their lands but cannot repair an irrigation canal? Why don't they sweep into the great cities and plunder the wealth of the rascals who buy their daughters and wives, who gorge on thirty-six course banquets while honest men starve? Why?"

Will nothing make a Chinese fight?

Why don't they stand up?

Will no-one come and lead them out of this?

Mr. Red Hair

Chingkangshan is wild country, untamed, its craggy volcanic peaks wreathed in fog for most of the year, its thick forests of pine, spruce and bamboo the lair of wolves, boars, tigers... It was into this wilderness that Mr. Twenty-eight Strokes led the tattered band which survived Chiang's extermination campaign and the Party's bungling.

Many years later, it will become famous as the shrine where he dreamed up the future and rewrote the book on the revolution.

Portraits of him painted in the Sixties show him then as a Christ-like figure aglow with a radiant intelligence and serene confidence: one such picture hung in the Vatican for many years where it was supposed to represent a Chinese missionary or even a Chinese version of Christ at the Second Coming. When its true subject was identified, it was hastily removed.

It wasn't like that: a more accurate picture would show him skinny from hunger, hair tangled, his faded gray jacket alive with lice, thick stubble concealing the mole on his chin: he is waiting by a cold mountain stream outside the miserable village they called Water Hole, expecting a visitor he knows he has to get on his side. His ragtag 'army' consists of only two thousand men, half of them bandits, robbers, runaway beggars, whores, vagabonds, armed with ancient swords and pitchforks. But Chu Teh, he knows, has at least a thousand men - with rifles - and Chu Teh is a military man and a very good one whereas he has never fired a gun in his life. And they need guns now. On the way here, they have seen what happens to those caught without them: in a field they found the bodies of twelve former comrades. Their skin had been stripped from them, their eyes gouged out and their ears and noses cut off. In a valley, the scattered bodies of seventeen young women lay half naked in the sun: they had all been raped and killed; one man must have been in a hurry because he'd taken the time to pull off only one leg of a girl's trousers.

As he scans the dark forest edge, shivering from the cold wind, a boy appears through the trees, waves his sword above his head, and then turns, gesturing a stocky man to pass.

Mao observes him: he is as they've described: short, compact, with big eyes and sensual lips, walking confidently but with no swagger. A crack Kuomintang general who'd amassed all the spoils - the palace, the harem, the finest black opium - he'd given it all away, the opium last because it was the hardest to kick. His method had already become a legend: when everything else failed, he took a steamer to Shanghai - a British steamer, knowing it would take a month and that they don't allow opium on their boats. When he got to Shanghai he was cured. It was then he decided to join the Party - exchange a poison for a medicine. He took a new name - Chu Teh, "Red Virtue" - though the Party wouldn't take him at first because he was poor at theory, so he went to Berlin where Chou En-lai let him join. When the Germans kicked him out, he came home, read some of Mao's pamphlets, and immediately understood what they meant.

Together they could change the world...

But first they must meet.

Chu Teh reaches the mountain stream, stops, stands on the other side. Mao says: "Welcome to Water Hole Soviet."

Chu Teh nods: "I have been sent to correct your errors."

But then a smile wipes the stern look from his face and he puts out a hand: "But they also say you're very good at defending yourself."

Mao helps him over the stream and they walk together up towards the village, its mud walls festooned with hand-written banners: "Long Live The Share-Wealth Party," "All Power to the Peasant-Soldier Alliance," "All Land to those who work it."

"And you?" says Mao, kicking a stone: "Do you think they are errors?"

"I am a soldier. I carry out orders."

"Yes, I know: it is how you lost Canton."

They pass a squad of soldiers sitting on bricks in the lee of a broken stone wall, talking earnestly in the cold morning sun, led by a young man with a cap sporting a red star. As they go by, Chu Teh can hear that the soldiers are criticizing one of their officers, though others praise him. The officer sits stone-faced, trying to blend into the wall, flushing red whenever they dare use his name.

A burst of noise - shouting and banging - makes them look up: an untidy, jostling crowd of peasants in ragged, quilted jackets and smeared, angry faces is approaching along the dusty village street, flanked by children beating gongs and yelling at a tall man wearing a pointed, white paper hat:

"Tyrant!" they yell at him, and spit:

"Bully!"

"Grain-hoarder!"

Mao and Chu Teh stand back to let the crowd pass:

"What will happen to him?"

Mao shrugs:

"If he recognizes his crimes, agrees to remodel his thinking, he can be saved; if not... Why kill a man when you can change his thinking? Please..." he gestures for Chu Teh to take a seat on one of the tree stumps arranged around a rough wooden table under a flowering cherry tree outside a simple peasant hut.

"So?" he says, lighting a cigarette: "tell me my errors."

"They say you are too soft on the peasants, you give them land instead of seizing it as state property. They want more burning and killing of class enemies. And they want you to march on Changsha."

"Yes, I know. And I will do it. Though we will be defeated."

"Then why...?" Chu Teh's forehead creases into a frown.

"It's the only way to get them to revise their thinking. They want to take cities - because that's what the books say - but this revolution will not begin in the cities; it will end there."

He pinches out his cigarette with his fingers, places the stub carefully on the table for later: "You understand: sometimes you have to lose a battle to win a war."

"Moscow says..."

Mao nods his head impatiently, reaches inside his trousers and pulls out a louse which he splits open with his long, dirty fingernails: "Sure, sure: when our foreign masters fart, we're expected to find it a lovely perfume."

"The Committee..."

"Yes, yes: you can't even go for a piss without a permit from a committee."

"They accuse you of localism, deviationism, revisionism..."

"And I them of opportunism, capitulationism, adventurism..."

They speak the terms seriously. Such words matter. They can cost you your life.

"And they don't like your flag, they say you've got no right to design your own flag."

Mao looks up at the torn but defiant banner fluttering from a tall pine tree: it depicts a hammer and sickle inside a big red star.

"What don't they like about it?"

"The star."

"Well, I'm not removing the star. I might remove the hammer..."

He picks up a twig and draws a big circle in the dust: "Look, this is China, and here..." he stabs at the edge of the circle, making little ragged dots along its perimeter: "these are the cities. It is only here China has any kind of proletariat - cowering under the guns of the Imperialists and their Chinese lackeys. But the cities rely on the peasants for food. Ninety percent of Chinese are peasants. Ninety percent of the government's income comes from peasants. Now you tell me: where would you raise your flag - here or here?"

Chu Teh is in full retreat by now and knows it, had expected it: "They say peasants have no class consciousness..."

"Then that is what we must give them. Listen: if they're not for us, there's no way we can win this thing."

"They say you yourself have a peasant consciousness."

"Yes," says Mao, and looks up at Chu Teh from underneath beetling eyebrows: "And you too, my friend, you too. We shouldn't be wasting time squabbling, you and I. The enemy is weak because of their squabbling. We should be planning how to do what we know has to be done."

He stands up: "A man is what he does; any fool can talk..."

Just then a young woman comes out of the hut bearing a plate of steaming rice, decorated with green squash and red peppers, a teapot of hot water and two mugs.

She is slim, a teenager, with fine hands and bright eyes like crystals. Mao's wife and two boys have stayed in Changsha. He hopes they'll be safe. He hasn't got time to worry about them now...

"I'm sorry," she says to Chu The, placing two wooden bowls on the table: "It's not much, but he has made a rule we are to eat only what the men eat."

"And with so many people starving in the North..." adds Mao, shoveling food into Chu Teh's bowl.

"Then you've heard about the famine? They say five million people will die..."

Mao just grunts.

"Shanghai has sent a group up there - with some food and leaflets. Not many, a dozen or so. Children most of them, teenagers..."

Mao scowls: "It's a waste. They'll only get themselves caught, tortured..."

And turns to his food. Yes, he's heard about the famine. It fed his quiet rage. He knows Chiang sent no relief to the starving because he feared his rolling stock would be seized by his rivals, whereas starvation would turn the people against them. It will always be that way so long as China is ruled by men more interested in holding power than using it to help the people, men for whom revolution means only their chance to gather plunder and power, rather than an opportunity to change the whole structure, the whole system, sweep away the old values, bring in the new.

He chews on his food, picking rice husks out of his teeth, picks up the cigarette stub, lights it: it doesn't have to be that way. Oh, he knows what the foreign press is saying, in their newspapers: that the Chinese peasant will never fight; well, let him tell them: the Chinese peasant has always been the one to rebel, to revolt. What do they know about the Red Eyebrows, or the Yellow Turbans, the Taiping - led by a man like him, a scholar from a peasant background? They only failed when they went to the cities, which corrupted them. Well, he isn't going to make that mistake.

He refills their mugs with hot water. He's got it all worked out: leave the cities 'til last; take the land, occupy an area you can not only conquer but also defend. And then: cancel all debts, abolish usury, tear up all deeds, smash the boundary stones, confiscate the land, give it to the peasants. Along with a gun: they'll fight. Hell, they need a revolution. All they want is something to believe in; all they want is hope...

But to do all this, he needs this man - who is also a peasant, and from Szechuan, which means he also likes hot red peppers in his belly.

Some of this he said to Chu Teh at that historic meeting in Water Hole Village. Most of it Chu Teh already knew: it was why he was here. Yes, it was unorthodox; yes, it offended classic Marxist doctrine: revisionist, deviationist... There was only one thing right about it: it could work.

Chu Teh gets up from the table and stretches his legs; he too is itching from too much sitting. Only one small event postpones their agreement and then only for a moment: the boy who stood guard at the forest edge appears in the village street. He has a girl with him - in a uniform several sizes too large. He is trying to be friendly, talk to her, but she won't even look at him. She walks straight up to Chu Teh, salutes; Chu Teh says: "Yes?" but the girl doesn't speak, darting suspicious looks at Mao. She has a face like a squirrel, sharp, pinched, mistrustful.

"It's all right," says Chu Teh kindly: "you can speak in front of Uncle."

She goes up to Chu Teh and whispers something in his ear, wary eyes still on Mao. Chu Teh grunts, says: "tell them I won't be long, we're nearly finished here." The girl walks away.

"So: you have women in your battalion too?"

"Yes. Fierce little devils. That one was picked up distributing leaflets; they must have done some pretty nasty things to her: she won't talk about it. When she came to us, her head was shaved raw. Now..."

You can see her little plaits swinging at the nape of her neck: to Mao, they look like a swallow's tail.

"If I join you," says Chu Teh: "our soldiers must be subject to the same rules. We have eight, very simple ones...

Mao says: "Replace doors after you leave a house; roll up the straw matting; speak politely; return anything you borrowed..."

Chu Teh nods: "Replace anything you've damaged; pay for what you take; bathe out of sight of women; don't search the pockets of captives."

They smile at each other; Mao says:

"And we must agree on tactics..."

"Yes."

"When the enemy advances," Mao begins,

"We retreat."

"When the enemy encamps..."

"We harass."

"When the enemy seeks to avoid battle,"

"We attack."

"When the enemy retreats,"

"We pursue..."

They nod solemnly; Mao says:

"Then shall we do this thing together? You and I...?"

"Yes." And then: "Do you think we should tell the Party?"

"They'll know soon enough. If it all works out the way I plan, they'll soon know about Chu-Mao."

"There is one thing," says Chu Teh, rebuckling his belt: "have you thought about going to Shanghai, telling your ideas to one of the foreign newspapermen there? They're free of censorship: they could publish..."

"Yes," says Mao, "But I'm not ready yet. Hell," he laughs: "I'm still making this up..."

A year later, their ranks swollen by deserters from the Kuomintang, by students and armed peasants, they take on Chiang's men and capture their first radio sets. A year later, they take twenty thousand prisoners and rifles; six months later, twenty thousand more rifles, several hundred machine guns and a hundred pieces of artillery, until they boast 200,000 men and 150,000 rifles and rule an area of two and a half million people.

Chiang calls in his German advisors and American bankers: it is time to wipe these bandits out once and for all.

And in Shanghai, the foreign newspapermen begin to ask about this new leader they're hearing about, this man called Mao-Chu:

"Mr. Red Hair...?"

We are taken to see our first commune. We are very quiet, very respectful. Huge sunflowers tower over the roofs, speckled faces measuring the distance they have to fall.

But it all seems to be going according to plan:

"Everyone gets the same wage," the cadre explains to us over tea and cigarettes: "everyone believes in the system and so everyone does their best."

Of course.

He feeds us luscious red water melons with black seeds which we spit out on the floor, shows us how Peking ducks are force-fed - with a funnel down their throat:

"In the old days," he jokes, "that's how students were taught. Now they're happy building the revolution."

"Are they too paid the same as everyone else?"

"Of course. We consider it an insult to offer a man a higher wage just because he's more gifted than others."

He does admit that the peasants have all been given private plots, and when we say "But isn't that dangerous, a reversion to capitalism?" he says that China is still a developing country:

"We are not yet a Communist society. During the Cultural Revolution some left-wing extremists tried to establish Communism overnight. This is called left-wing infantile adventurism: it is not correct and they were severely criticized for it."

We know who he means: although Jiang Qing herself is lying low for now, her protégés run the newspapers: Yao Wen-yuen and Zhang Chun-qiao are the "two cocks" to her "hen." It was they who hatched the eggs of the Cultural Revolution by attacking a play she didn't like, and then drafted the most radical plan of all - to return to the origins of the Revolution, turn China into a decentralized federation of independent, self-sufficient communes.

They say Mao himself put a stop to that, but they haven't gone away, are waiting for the winds to shift.

So are we.

Meanwhile, they take us out to the Great Wall and point at the spot Nixon reached. We, of course, go past it, to the top, but are a bit blinded by the sun.

On the way back, the road passes through farmland: schoolchildren squat in the hot vegetable fields among the purple aubergines and red peppers, for it is harvest time. Maize stands rigid awaiting execution, brittle skin peeled back to expose the yellow brain cells, red tassels dangling like veins. Children march along the side of the road holding little sickles, but I don't see any hammers. They wear red armbands. Red Guards?! Our guides say "Yes" but reorganized, sent to work in the fields two days a week to learn from the peasants.

Strange: I thought the peasants were the ones supposed to be doing the learning: how to give up their Confucian conservatism, their selfish hunger for their own land...?

Children also sweep the streets every morning and clean out the public latrines, because a revolution is not won during its violent phase - that is only for power; it is won afterwards, in the minds and hearts of its children. I hope they understand that they're doing this so as to learn that all forms of labour are equal in dignity, because otherwise it is just child labour.

While we stand looking at them wonderingly, one of the Chinese teachers hunts in the flowers by the side of the road and finds a cricket for Tracey. It has a red, jeweled spot in the middle of its forehead and when she puts it in a box of leaves, it chirps a melancholy song of nostalgia for the lost sun. By the time we get home it has sung itself out and lies dead in the bottom of the leafy box, the red jewel on its forehead now a dull brown.

Meanwhile, back at the Friendship Guesthouse, I join a study group. There are about twenty of us in the small room and at first everyone just talks freely but then Elizabeth from Austria interrupts and says this is too formless: when someone wants to speak they should put up their hand. The way we are doing it, she says, is "anarchistic spontaneity." A Swedish woman agrees with her: since we are discussing the dictatorship of the proletariat, she says, we should exercise group discipline. I pipe up that I am a proletarian and that discipline is not the prerogative of any one class, to which Elizabeth replies that that smacks to her of "liberal eclecticism."

I go on to talk about Worker's Control, the Yugoslav Model, and am accused of being a revisionist and deviationist.

"How can I be a revisionist when I'm not even a proper Marxist?"

She looks shocked and promises to give me some books to help me with my problem.

When things like this happen, I wander out to the commune attached to the Institute: I love it out here, it renews my faith. It's not much to look at: a huddle of low, mud-walled houses with delicate, fretted paper windows. Along the side of the road, stubborn leaves cling to the poplar trees like little brown bats, dreaming of eternal spring. Out in the fields, the cabbages which escaped the harvest regret it now, lying in the hard fields, frost-bitten, pinched black, runny with bad colds. A little red tractor moves jerkily across the field, turning the soil before it freezes: the winter wheat will lie frozen in the ground until the spring comes to release it.

These fields were once Manchu burial grounds: marble memorial slabs squat among the carrots and it is impossible to tell how much is earth and how much is human dust, so much is soil and how much is human sweat. Grannies hold babies with snotty noses, a boy scratches a pig with a stick, his sister grinding almonds and orange skin with herbs and honey, for it is the season of coughs.

I stop and chat with the peasants and they happily show me their new litter of piglets, offer me sunflower seeds, even show me their houses, which they have built themselves at an average cost of two hundred dollars.

A donkey cart lumbers by, its driver lolling asleep over his contented belly: my nose tells me it's a night-soil cart. Cadres who were criticized in the Cultural Revolution were often assigned to drive them - for their re-education and as part of a campaign to make it an honorable profession, since all work should be evaluated on the basis of social benefit and there is nothing more valuable than shit.

On the edge of the lake the reeds bend in the wind...

III

Back in Shanghai, Ed tried not just to postpone the predestined meeting in the distant hills but walk away from it altogether.

Frustrated, irritable, chain-smoking his way through the chilly, damp streets, sensing that time was passing and his ambitions unfulfilled, he tried to get away. He thought of going to Russia but his visa application was refused because of J.B.'s anti-Soviet stance. Not for the last time, Ed was guilty by association. He even contemplated returning to America, writing his brother to inquire if he knew of any good job in advertising in New York City. Ironically, it was the stock market crash that shattered that option.

By now he was filing copy not just for The Review but also as roving correspondent for The New York Sun and The Chicago Daily News, and legman for The New York Herald Tribune. They weren't interested in political pieces, only in travel articles, adventure stories, but it was one way to get out and so he went down to Canton and Hanoi, Hong Kong and Macao. He tried to flush out the filth of the cities by following Marco Polo's route through the steamy jungles of Burma where he got malaria and fell in love with his gentle nurse. Then on to India to see if Gandhi's peaceful alternative could replace the escalating inevitability of violent revolution.

Sometimes, at night, wandering some lonely street, the girl's eyes would well up from his subconscious and shame him, but he drowned them in the cathouses of Tokyo geishas and Vietnamese courtesans.

It all backfired.

The signposts on his road to himself all pointed backwards.

In Hanoi he found not relief but rebellion - and the colonial response to it: not fear but petulant exasperation: "How dare the natives be so ungrateful?" The Vietnamese were asking for the abolition of serfdom, polygamy and the puppet monarchy; the French response was to bring out the guillotine.

"They may care little for this life," scoffed one French diplomat: "but they are terrified of the idea of facing the next as a headless ghost."

They censored his stories, but he smuggled them out through Hong Kong:

"New heads," he predicted, "will grow from the torsos of the fallen leaders. They will always be waiting - for French vigilance to weaken, for France to be involved in major troubles elsewhere, waiting for arms, for the next world war, tirelessly waiting..."

Ed hoped that his revelations about Vietnam would affect US policy, but back home no-one was listening; he realized that if he was going to exert any influence, he needed to beat his stories up, mix the yeast of publicity into the daily bread of his writing. It wasn't a moral problem: Ed knew that you don't just write stories, you have to sell them.

In India, the 'leper in the diaper' turned him off with his prissy self-righteousness and prim views on sexual abstinence, Ed noting caustically that Gandhi had conveniently postponed his own celibacy until after he'd sired a large family.

Instead he discovered Marxism. Along with the Bhagavad Gita and the Kama Sutra, it was in India that he first read Marx, Lenin, Engels - into whose seductive secrets he was initiated by friendly, young Indian radicals.

But he was stunned - and cross - to find that consorting with them had prompted the Indian CID to open a dossier on him in which he figured as a dangerous Red, ex-convict and opium smuggler, traveling on a false passport as an agent of the Comintern! Nothing came of it - except a delay in filing his stories and Ed's exasperation that mere association with radicals could question the chastity of his journalistic ethics.

After a year away, he realized that he was homesick - and that it was for China.

Back in Shanghai, he began to write more about the suffering he saw around him - and the incompetence of the Kuomintang. He had become a bit of a loner. Why did he respond with distressed compassion when everyone else protected themselves with sneering disdain? Ed was one of those people who, when they see something wrong, wonder what the solution might be. The foreign journalists in the bar of the Palace Hotel knew that there wasn't one, not for China, whose ills they ascribed to some racial flaw, some genetic passivity and cynical fatalism. But everywhere else in the world, nations were rallying behind charismatic leaders; Ed didn't like them, but China needed one. Where is he? What about this new man: Mr. Red Hair?

"In full retreat, buddy, marched off West. No way through there: only monkeys can get over those mountains."

He went to a small left-wing bookshop and bought some tracts, not knowing that the bright-eyed girl who served him would soon be sleeping with Mao in Chingkanshan, any more than he could know that one of the actresses in a street theatre performance demonstrating against an American movie on Nanjing Road was one Lan Ping - who would soon change her name to Jiang Qing and replace Zizhen in Mao's affections when he finally fought his way to Yenan.

The signposts were all there: he just couldn't read them yet.

But he did deepen his own education in tragedy: when the Yangtze flooded, he went up to see. Two million people had drowned and millions more been left homeless and destitute. The desolation reminded him of the famine, but his tone was different now. He had written up the famine as a compassionate foreign observer; now he tried to see it through the eyes of a Chinese peasant in all his agony, despair and sullen fury. The flood was not a natural disaster but "the outcome of a long series of afflictions" caused by extortionate taxes, looting soldiers and absentee landlords "trembling now before the long range and thrust of the wild new cry of Communism." He castigated the Kuomintang for their "callous indifference, tyrannous oppression and ruinous incompetence. I have seen so much pain and suffering that it has entered my own blood."

When the Japanese invaded Manchuria, hungry for its mines and timber, he again had to go up and see it all for himself. There were dead Chinese everywhere, their courage in the face of certain defeat "the most heroic thing I have seen."

Perhaps China could and would stand up after all...

He had to leave prematurely, bedridden with sinusitis contracted in the freezing cold of the North, but that meant that he was in the right place when the Japanese moved down on Shanghai itself.

Having advance word of the impending assault from an interview with the Japanese commander, Ed shelved his journalist's scruples about non-intervention and hurried to North Station to warn the station manager to disperse the Chinese, waiting, patient as ever, on the platforms with their baskets of fresh fish and crickets in wicker cages. The station manager eventually agreed - though more out of concern to save his trains than the people. On the way back to the safety of the Settlement, Ed witnessed the Japanese marines advancing along Jukong Road and the first Chinese casualty. "The first shots of World War Two," he called it when his eyewitness dispatch appeared as the banner story on page one of The Chicago Daily News and The New York Sun. Though the editors changed his lead - "The streets of Shanghai are red with blood tonight" - they cabled congratulations on his scoop. Buoyed by this success, he went up on the ramparts built in the sixteenth century to keep out Japanese pirates, watched the Japanese air raids on civilian targets, then slipped down into the streets where the Chinese, to everyone's surprise, weren't just laying down their arms and fleeing but resisting.

For five weeks, Ed scurried back and forth across the lines, picking his way across the bomb craters and naked, roasted bodies; twice he was arrested and once shot at by a Chinese sniper who put a hole in his hat. He came across the fresh corpse of a fallen Japanese aviator "just after a Chinese soldier had pulled out his smoking heart, leaving a deep dark wound the shape of a perfect cross."

He was protected by his press card but found the price he had to pay for his immunity was heavy, forced to watch, helpless to intervene, as a troop of Japanese soldiers herded Chinese civilians out of their homes into a bamboo thicket, which they then set on fire. He did manage to rescue one young girl who he found wandering distraught when her father had been shot down, and another whose leg and hand had been blown off.

But the Japanese wanted only Chinese Shanghai, leaving the International Settlement to drown out the bombing with Rudi Vallee. It's not my war, he told himself. Though impressed by the Chinese resistance, his cynicism was fed by the way the Nineteenth Route Army - which had put up the most heroic defense - was liquidated when Chiang found out it contained a high proportion of Communists.

Ed retreated again: he would exorcise those haunting, challenging eyes once and for all. A young American woman had come to see him - the very day she arrived in Shanghai, two beaux carrying her golf bag and tennis racquets. She'd read everything Ed had ever written, could quote his own words back at him. Her name was Helen Foster - "but my friends all call me Peg." She was from Utah where she'd studied China and decided, she said, "to put on my roller skates and come out and become the Empress of Asia."

"It takes an emperor to make an empress," said Ed, flirting, attracted by her energy, her brash freshness - not to mention a trim body and "dancing blue eyes."

Peg was soon surrounded by a court of lecherous admirers but she rebuffed them all: "I've turned down twenty one marriage proposals already," she confided to Ed: "My only passion is to be a writer. I plan to write travel books and at least one good novel." The only hindrance she could see was her bland name, so Ed helped her compose a new one - "like they do here:" "Nym" from Shakespeare, "Wales" from her parents' homeland. He offered to show her the sights and, as a cock crowed and the vultures burped, "we ate rapturous food under green willows and in tranquil temple pavilions; took long walks across the rice field pathways and through mulberry groves in the silk country, and sailed the blue lakes on dragon junks under arched bridges along the Grand Canal in the moonlight." They talked, endlessly: Peg was a straight-A student whose mother had been a suffragette; she had very simple solutions for the problems of China: "I have an instinct," she said, "for getting other people to bestir themselves. All China needs is a good push from behind." She declined to read Marx - "not the type of thing an all-American girl would find inspiring" - or learn Chinese: "they tell me it damages your brain-cells." Anyway, Japan, she assured Ed, would make a good ruler of China - better than Westerners and better than the Chinese too: "It is only fitting that an Eastern country now inherit the mandate the West has enjoyed and not known how to use." That problem solved, they turned to the "large abstract questions such as what is truth, where do the senses end and reason begin, what is reality and what is illusion." The elusive panacea, they decided, would be some way "to combine 'the sense power of the West,' its vigor developed by the repressive teachings and ideas of sin inherent in Judeo-Christianity, with the 'brain power of China,' its senses atrophied by over-indulgence in sex."

They resolved that issue their own way: they got married, Peg insisting that it be in "nice and clean Tokyo." She made Ed exchange the ill-fitting lavender pinstripe suit he'd bought in India for fashionable Harris Tweeds with padded shoulders, and they spent their honeymoon cruising the Southern Seas on a Japanese freighter: "the air was soft and warm, the sea a sheet of shimmering silk." Then on to Bali, which, for a while, even reconciled Ed to Imperialism: there was no violence, no beggars, no starvation; even the pigs were scrubbed clean.

But his doubts would not lie down. He found the Japanese on the freighter scornful and arrogant: the richest parts of Asia, they told him over dinner, had not been efficiently exploited by the white masters: "Look at how little you Americans have achieved in the Philippines compared to the progress and prosperity of Formosa under Japanese rule."

As for Bali, Ed sensed that Paradise is not for export and that it too was ultimately doomed. There are snakes in the Gardens of Eden. In the end, what he took away with him was the lesson of their communal organization, their practice of selfless co-operation founded on a shared set of values, a shared ideology in which all individual effort is for the common good:

"In Bali I learned that it is just as 'natural' for people to work together as it is for them to be mutually predatory. That was a great lesson to learn in 1933."

Communalism: Communism? You don't have to sit for years in the British Museum Library to understand that we love ourselves best when we love those around us. But the answer didn't lie in the British Museum, or in Bali: Ed knew that the answer - his answer, and perhaps the world's or at least the poor half of it - lay in China. J.B. had said it: "You'll be back. China - not India or Russia - is going to be the great story of our generation." And he, Ed, was going to write it. In 1933, Ed and Peg packed up their house and moved to Peking: they would unlock the secret of China, go back to the roots: Shensi, cradle of the Chinese race, Sian, Yenan - where, they heard, people lived in caves...

It had been a long detour. Ed never went to Australia but if he had, he'd have learned that the Aborigines regularly go on a "walkabout," first at puberty and then later - whenever they feel lost.

They learn who they were in the Dreamtime, and so become who they once dreamed they would be.

Walkabout Two

The Long March was not premeditated; it was improvised: a snaking detour, six thousand miles long.

But it is by circuitous rotes that we come home to our selves.

Confucius might say 'A man should walk straight and never bend,' but Lao-tze knew better, and Mao-Lao-Tao is more than a clever rhyme. 'Water is the strongest thing, it can wear down stone' and so they followed Lao-tze: they flowed where the water finds ways through the rocks that the rocks can do nothing about.

It is by improvisation that we get better at being who we are.

On October 16th 1934, they load sewing machines, printing presses, boxes of documents and books on mules and donkeys and set off, each man bearing a coolie shoulder pole on which he hangs two boxes of ammunition, hand grenades and a can of kerosene. In his pack each man has a drinking cup and three pairs of cloth shoes with rope soles tipped and heeled with metal; a pair of chopsticks stuck in his puttees and a needle and thread jabbed on the underside of his peaked cap. They wear big sun-hats made of layers of bamboo and oiled paper. Little do they know that they will march for a year, cross the deepest and most dangerous rivers of China, climb its highest mountains, tramp through shivering cold and withering heat, through wind and snow and rainstorm, wracked by typhus, malaria, dysentery, trachoma, iodine deficiency, cholera, meningitis... A few will get syphilis but they are very young, very tired, and there are only a hundred women among them.

One of these is Chu Teh's courier, sent to Mao with a message that he's been delayed, has been kidnapped by one of Mao's Party rivals. She wants to return, but is cut off: she carries a gun now and a dagger in her belt, warning to friend and foe alike that she doesn't just shoot her enemies, or her suitors: she scalps them.

Mao leads the way, carrying an umbrella, his books on a horse; he is accompanied by Zizhen, who he married after his wife and sister were captured by the Kuomintang, tortured and executed.

It takes them six months to reach the Tatu River. It is the climax: Chiang is waiting for them. Here they can still lose everything. Emerging from the forests that have sheltered them from Kuomintang spotter planes, they look down and see with amazement and delight that one of the ferryboats is tethered on their side of the river. No-one has been expecting them for weeks yet. Sixteen volunteers offer to seize the boat, cross the river and bring back the other two. The river is in roaring spring flood but, by starting upstream, they manage to reach the other shore, scale the steep cliffs and turn their machinegun on the enemy below, shattering their mahjong tiles.

For three days the three boats work round the clock, but the current is too turbulent: at this rate it will take them weeks to ferry the whole army across and already Kuomintang planes are circling like patient vultures.

But they cannot fail now: already they have scaled Old Mountain along narrow paths and across icy streams, the path so steep you could see the sole of the man ahead. They have crossed the Wu river on rafts contrived of bamboo and skin, captured the ferry at Tsunyi by dressing up in enemy uniforms and then burning the boats behind them. They have crossed the Yangtze, skirted the Burmese border, drunk blood oaths with fierce Lolo tribesmen, swearing that whoever breaks them will be reborn as a weak and cowardly chicken. They have climbed over Fire Mountain where no tree or bush or blade of grass grows and they have to drink their own urine for lack of water. But the Chairman tells them how Monkey had climbed over this one on his way to India to collect Buddhist scriptures: "the heat singed the hairs off his behind," he says: "which is why monkeys today have bare bottoms."

They can't lose it all now...

Mao is gaunt and grumpy, constipated from chronic bowel disorder, exacerbated by a diet of roots, fungus, pine cones and grass. He needs some red peppers to unblock this obstacle, but up here he might as well ask for an American cigarette. Every herb they have passed on the way he's tried to dry and smoke, and now he tries out his latest improvisation. He knows this area - not personally but from books: it was at this very spot that his heroes of the "Romance of the Three Kingdoms" had met their end, and the last of the Taiping rebels were put to death by slicing. Local legend says you can still hear their spirits cry out for revenge.

"Over there," he points West: "about hundred miles, where the gorges rise high and the river runs deep, there is an iron-chain suspension bridge. The Bridge That Liu Built. It is the last crossing

East of Tibet. If we can take it, we will be safe."

He does not bother to say what will happen if they fail.

A select company of barefoot Reds, including a few women, sets out through the winding gorges, waist-deep mud and thick fog. At the same time, the battalion which crossed by ferry moves along the Northern bank; sometimes the gorge is so narrow they can shout to each other; at other times the gulf is so wide it seems it might separate them for ever. Forced-marching through the night by the light of torches fabricated from straw fences, they pause only for ten-minute rests when the political cadres move among them, explaining over and again the importance of this action, exhorting each to march until he drops.

The Bridge That Liu Built is made of thirteen heavy iron chains, each link the size of a rice bowl, with a span of a hundred meters straddling the cascading river, the ends embedded under great piles of cemented rock. Thick planks lashed across the chains make the bridge, but half of them have been removed: midway over the torrent, only nine bare chains swing in the mist. An enemy machinegun nest occupies the Northern bridgehead: they haven't bothered to destroy the chains - how can anyone get across?

Too many volunteers step forward, competing for the task. Twenty-two are selected. Hand grenades, swords and Mausers strapped to their backs, they swing hand over hand over the boiling waters. Snipers pick them off; one and then another falls to his death, but then one reaches the planks on the other side and, hanging by one hand, lobs his hand grenade into the enemy redoubt. Desperately the enemy pours paraffin over the remaining planks and sets fire to it, but now a dozen Reds, some with their hair on fire, are crawling towards them on their hands and knees.

The enemy retreats - throwing down their rifles, terrified of these superhuman, fiery daemons - into the arms of the Red battalion which has now arrived along the Northern bank.

A week later, they move on, but not before doing what they always do: destroying land deeds, abolishing taxes, freeing slaves, calling mass meetings, setting up a soviet protected by the partisans and political teachers they leave behind them, for this is not just war, this is liberation, revolution.

There is only one thing wrong with this story: suppose it never gets told...?

Mao wants to send Chu Teh's courier back to get reinforcements and tell him where they are, but no-one knows where he is: reluctantly she obeys the order to move on, followed by a young man who tries to introduces himself as Lao Kou - "Old Dog" - but is greeted only by a growl.

Another two thousand miles stretch before them, studded by seven mountain ranges. Many die from exposure on the Great Snowy Mountain and Paotung Kang Mountain where they build a bamboo road over waist-deep mud, are battered by hail the size of potatoes and attacked by Tibetans who use their own tactics against them, stripping houses bare, carrying off all food, rolling down huge boulders on them as they march through the narrow passes, opposed by a Queen who has threatened that anyone who helps these Chinese invaders will be boiled alive. One day Mao will come back and settle that score too, but there are still the terrible Grasslands to cross, an endless sea of tall, razor-sharp grass drenched with perpetual rain, crisscrossed by a maze of narrow paths where many lose their lives, sucked down, helplessly struggling, into the stinking, icy, black mud. Lao Kou scavenges for raw wheat, rats, dead horses and green turnips which give them diarrhea. They sleep standing up, the girl reluctantly allowing him to lean against her back. In a deserted tribal village he discovers an altar with bowls of sacrificial food - nuts, dates, rice and cheese - and, wonder of wonders, figurines of gods, which, under the green and red paint, turn out to be made of wheat and butter!

On October 20th 1935, they straggle into the safety of Shensi, more skeletons than men.

Only one in twenty has made it.

The Long March is one story where you don't have to beat up the facts. They fought over 300 skirmishes and 15 pitched battles, marched for 243 of the 368 days, averaging one halt for every 114 miles of marching. They crossed eighteen mountain ranges, twenty-four rivers and broke through the enveloping armies of ten warlords as well as the combined might of the Kuomintang, in the process turning a demoralizing retreat into a march towards certain victory. It is hard not to adopt an epic tone faced by one of the greatest military feats in history and the greatest Exodus since the children of Israel left Egypt: a thousand tales of courage, sacrifice, loyalty, proof that the human will can survive every challenge thrown down by nature or fellow-man, and never admit defeat. To tell it properly one would have to tell the individual story of every single man and woman: Chen Yi who had himself roped to a tree while they poured Tiger Balm into the putrid wound in his thigh; Li Teh weeping in pain as he unwinds the tattered bandages from his lacerated feet, the only shoes he has worn for six months; Ho Lung shoveling salt into his mouth from a captured warehouse like it was sugar. How do you get people to do things like this? They have inspired leaders, of course, and good luck with their enemies, but they have something else. Mao knows that you can give people land, you can cancel their debts, tear up their land deeds, put a chicken in every pot, but in the end what they want is something less tangible and more precious. Hope. Belief. A dream, which becomes a vision, which comes true. For once, reality rises to the call of a vision and does not let it down.

It doesn't happen often: reality can't stand too many ideals.

Arriving in Shensi, Mao summons Lin Piao, Deng Xiao-ping, Chou En-lai, Liu Shao-chi and the others he has forged into what has become the most hardened fighting force in China.

They all line up and, solemnly, have a piss together.

Then he wanders off, alone except for his batman.

The others turn away.

It is a well-oiled routine.

At a discrete distance, Mao stops, lowers his trousers, bends forward and his batman sticks a finger up his anus. Sniffing a piece of dried human sewage he has picked up from a field, Mao squats and waits.

"There goes Chiang," he grunts.

Pushing down hard like a pregnant peasant woman giving birth, he growls:

"And here comes Japan."

He pulls up his trousers: that's better. Now I wonder if there's a journalist, a Western reporter able to tell this story...?

He sleeps that night in a cave cut into the side of a hill made of yellow soil blown down from the Gobi desert. In the morning, he takes out his brushes, wets them in his mouth, grinds black ink with saliva on a stone and writes a poem:

"This northern scene:
A thousand leagues locked in ice,
A myriad leagues of fluttering snow...
A sunny day is needed
To see them, with added elegance,
In red and white."

He pauses, waiting for the next verse to form itself in his mind and flow out through the hairs of his brush, but he already has a name for it: he calls it simply "Snow."

I have given up a lot to be here: back in Berkeley, I lived the good life - intelligent, witty friends with whom to discuss the big questions, a beautiful wife, an apartment with a sauna. We'd go horse-riding in the hills, buy cheap wine in the Napa Valley and eat in small restaurants in Chinatown. I was assured of tenure, rapid promotion, a comfortable retirement, was popular with the students who found my Cockney accent sexy rather than a source of shame. But it was as if my life was already over, that I could already write the last page, close the book.

I have come here to escape academia, to escape its seductions. I'd started to get scared that this was as good as it gets, wondered if I should write a novel, pour all the irritable dissatisfaction and vague yearnings into fiction. Instead I fled to Asia, spent time in India, Bali, wrote books about their theatre. There was much there to be seduced by - and to make one angry, but I was always a foreigner, always a tourist, never had to feel any sense of responsibility. Even when I took up Chinese it was to learn calligraphy, not speak it; even when I first read Mao, it was his poetry. I think I came here because I have, in the end, a guilty conscience, feel I should somehow be involved. My Ph. D. was on Ibsen and already I'd found inspiration there: Nora's "I have to find out who's right, the world or me," Stockmann's "The most important thing is not to have to spit at your own image:" these I'd paste up on my shaving mirror. In Berkeley, I gathered a group together and we did some street theatre: staged a mock funeral for American democracy along Telegraph Avenue, put on pig-face masks and taunted the National Guard sent in to break up the "Free Speech Movement," built an imitation Vietnamese village in the middle of the football stadium and then set fire to it...

Our models were the Russian Living Newspapers of the Thirties, and the People's Theatre Companies in China. Red Star Over China has a chapter in which Ed Snow gives a vivid description of agit-prop theatre in the liberated Soviets around Yenan. That was when I first read him, and then Hinton, Robinson, all the other Westerners who wrote so admiringly about what was happening in China. When I first heard about the Cultural Revolution, it was enough to make any theatre director eat his heart out: a cast of millions, acting out a national drama, in which a new type of human being was to be born. If I couldn't write something like that myself, or direct it, I wanted at least to be a spectator and even an actor... Wasn't Jiang Qing, Mao's wife, an actress; didn't she replace Ed Snow as Mao's publicist - and, they whisper, is even making a bid now to succeed Mao himself?

Because what's really seductive about theatre is that you have to put it on, turn the ideas into actions, the visions into flesh and blood. That's the challenge; that's the problem: one of my former colleagues, Willy Willetts, an expert on Chinese pottery, published a book on it and was told by his editor to use the royalties to go to China.

He declined:

"I already have my China," he said: "In my head. I like it - just the way it is."

IV

Ed was very close now.

There was one last temptation. China has other ways to divert you than sing-song girls, opium clouds, and lotus roots for breakfast: the world's longest-running tragedy is also the world's oldest continuous civilization - with a literature, philosophy, poetry, architecture and art to occupy you for many a lifetime. And it is all in Peking, especially at the Universities. If roaming about as a tourist is a way to see a country without knowing it, academia is its complement: a way of knowing without seeing. In Peking the houses all face inwards - on a central courtyard where trimmed plants in ceramic pots replace the wild unpredictability of nature, and caged birds sing of a freedom they will never know.

Ed and Peg had three such houses - the first in Mei Cha Hutong: six rooms, with a bath, a walled compound of willows and fruit trees and servant quarters. Its gates were of red lacquer behind which was a dragon screen to keep out ghosts and evil spirits who, as everyone knows, travel only in straight lines. I tracked that one down and visited it myself: it had become a shabby, crowded place, home to six families, but it's the one I would have wanted to live in if, when I was there, you were allowed to choose where to live - which you weren't. On the other hand, if - like Ed at that time - you were a scholar-writer like me seeking political action, it could have been counter-productive: a place for introspection rather than intervention, a place to speculate rather than participate. Neither of us was there for that.

In 1934 they moved out to the village of Haidian - to be near Yenching University where Ed landed a part-time job in the journalism department. It was a retirement villa complete with swimming pool and a picture window overlooking the Summer Palace. But he had begun to fret: it felt sometimes as if his life was already over and had somehow never happened. This, he said to himself, is how retired people live. He was not a good lecturer, weighing his papers down with citations and abstractions, so unlike the vivid, anecdotal quality of personal experience and human detail which enlivened his newspaper work. He edited a volume of Chinese short stories: is this all I am, a waiter at the table of life? Laid low with malarial fever and a bout of dysentery, he lay in his bed shivering, scared that, somewhere along the line, he'd taken a wrong turning, had brushed against a burning bush and not even realized it. His book on the Japanese annexation of Manchuria - called prophetically Far Eastern Front - had sold only seven hundred copies. In it he foresaw accurately the inevitability of a major conflict between Japan and the Western powers: "it will take a world war to stop them now." But no-one at home was listening: the Nips could strut over China but no American was scared of slit-eyed, bow-legged pygmies. He jotted down notes for another book. He knew what kind of a story he wanted to write, or at least the ingredients: hope, for a world drifting into the arms of Fascist thugs; belief, for a world betrayed too many times.

He was trapped in the classic cul-de-sac of the sympathetic outsider: something must be done; but they must do it.

Perhaps he should write a novel, a love-story, pour it all out into fiction - the yearning, the passion...

So they moved house again, back to the city. Adjacent to the ancient East Wall, this one had steam heat, marble baths, a tennis court and stables. Ed converted the garden greenhouse into his study. They went horse riding in the hills, swam in the pool at the American Legation, got their wine cheap from the Italian monastery, had their own cook, a private rickshaw and affected long, silk-padded, Chinese gowns. They weren't rich but "where else can a freelance correspondent live like a bank president?"

An unexpected advance of $750 for a book kept them for a year. It was to be on the Chinese Communist Movement: "it will need original research, and at least one visit to an important Red area. That's the problem: the Red Army has been squeezed by Chiang's latest annihilation campaign. By all reports they've marched off

West. Anyway," he added in conclusion: "a Marxist revolution can't happen here until the industrialization of Japan-occupied Manchuria creates a proletarian leadership for the backward peasantry..."

Peg was happy. Peking was so different from Shanghai - even the rickshaw men were polite and spoke Mandarin. Starvation and revolution seemed remote and unreal among the whisky-sodas and tennis. She had calling cards engraved, learned which corner to turn down, and they did the rounds of the tea-parties, receptions, antique-shops and polo matches. Peg was soon thoroughly at home in the circle of Chinese intellectuals, foreign diplomats, missionaries, journalists and expatriate scholars, enjoying spirited debates with Teilhard de Chardin, Pearl Buck and the Swedish explorer Sven Hedin who gave them a beautiful white greyhound they christened Gobi. When the dust blew down from the desert, they took refuge in the study of Chinese art and philosophy, but Ed soon came to the conclusion that the energy needed to learn all this could mean you'd have none left to use what you learned. He did take Chinese lessons, realizing that Chinese history and psychology are embedded in their script, fascinated to find that the Chinese picto-graph for love "is made up of three characters meaning bird in flight, heart, and man walking with dignity and grace." But he never saw himself as the latter and felt his own wings had been clipped. He managed to master 1,500 characters so as not to be a total "blind man" as the Chinese call illiterates, but concluded that the difficulty of ever learning to write it must be a conspiracy to keep the real secrets from outsiders.

He bought a Japanese-made bike which he found "superior in every respect" as a way of getting around Peking.

But, like every other apparent detour, this one too led eventually and inexorably to the red star rising in the North. For though Mao is right that the Chinese rebel has always come from the peasantry, in our time, revolutions have always been started by students. China was no exception, and in Peking, Ed met the students; more, he joined them.

And one of them had a direct line to Mao...

Ed first heard of Mao from no less than Soong Qing-ling, the most revered woman in China, widow of Sun Yat-sen who had led the 1912 Revolution and who she married in a fit of adolescent hero-worship. Ousted by the warlords and betrayed by Chiang, Sun died broken-hearted, leaving his young wife to keep the flame alive and pure. Ed called her "the conscience and constant heart of the still unfinished revolution."

They met first in Shanghai when he did a profile on her for The New York Herald Tribune. Her house in the Rue Molière was constantly guarded and watched by Kuomintang plainclothesmen and French police, so they met in the American hangout called The Chocolate Shop on Bubbling Well Road - the very same place he'd first met Peg. Madame Soong spoke perfect English, had been educated in America - at Wesleyan College: "my friends call me Suzie." She was everything Ed admired in a woman: beautiful, educated, slender, courageous. They became friends: she gave Ed and Peg a silver electric coffee percolator for their wedding, but they never could get it to work on Chinese current. She knew more about the Chinese political scene than anyone else, her sister having married Chiang Kai-shek when she herself turned down his proposal, and her brother being his banker. These family connections did not cloud her political judgment: Chiang was corrupt, a murderer, his regime a betrayal of her husband's visions...

"And the Communists?"

They were sitting in her modest salon, among the scrolls and flowers, Aida on the gramophone, her jet hair pulled back in a bun secured by a jade hairpin, which she reached up and adjusted:

"What do you think?" she countered.

"I'm not sure they're even real Communists. Just men who've been crushed, oppressed, robbed, bullied. I can understand them looting and pillaging the towns, ravaging the countryside, killing the upper classes. I guess it'll take some such destructive peasant violence to bring down the old order, but I don't know they have much idea what to put in its place. My fear is that if they ever do come to power, it will mean the triumph of mob rule. They don't have the proper ideological background," Ed concluded: "How can they: there isn't even a translation into Chinese of Marx's Capital, is there?"

"Perhaps we're still writing our own version ourselves," she said gently. "It's not something I can discuss openly with you. Even to speak about Communism is a crime. Only two years ago many of my young friends were arrested, made to dig their own graves, bound, thrown in the pits and buried alive. Evidently in his Bible studies our Christian Generalissimo never reached Corinthians."

"Is there any leader in China you trust?"

"I mistrust Mao Zedong least of all."

Ed wrote the name down.

"Perhaps…" he said, looking up, hopefully: "I mean: is there any way I could meet him, this Mr. Mao? Better still, if I could get behind the lines, see for myself…"

Soong Qing-ling said nothing, got up and changed the record.

She did tease him - gently: when Ed said that the only way he could see of denying Japan the rights of colonial conquest enjoyed by the West was for the West to give them away voluntarily, she said:

"Ah, Mr. Snow, but your extraterritorial rights include freedom from censorship. A Chinese would be executed for saying the sorts of things you can freely write."

"Touché, but do you know there's a police dossier on me - in which I'm depicted as a friend of radicals and a subversive? Things like that do me no good in my work: no editor in America is going to publish the views of a Commie sympathizer."

"Then we must make sure you stay clean."

Ed wasn't sure what she meant by that. He couldn't know that, the next morning, she wrote a letter: she had been Dr. Sun's cryptographer and knew all about secret codes and inks…

Not that there were any Communists to contaminate Ed in Peking. The students called themselves radicals, but they were the sons and daughters of Westernized, urban businessmen and professionals.

Idealistic, patriotic, they took seriously the Confucian ethic that the scholar is the voice of China's moral and political conscience, who should speak up, even against an Emperor. Some of Ed's students were refugees from Manchuria and all of them were left-wing: it was the chic thing to be, it made you popular, and your family connections kept Chiang's thugs at bay. The boys sported American-style slacks and pullovers and the girls rode around demurely in their slit skirts on bicycles. They were delicate, well-bred, with short hair and pale skin: they would meet in the Snows' house where they could read his foreign newspapers, talk freely, earnestly while Ed served them coffee and wine and listened in:

"Fascism is the last gasp of Capitalism;"

"Revolution is the only vote we have;"

"Proletarian dictatorship is only a temporary evil on the way to a classless society..."

To them, Communism was a debating topic. With one exception: one day a tall, pale, handsome boy wearing an unkempt gown turned up at the Snow's regular Wednesday discussion group. Ed as usual was sitting to one side, reserving his judgment, but Peg as usual was wading in, talking like a machine-gun, castigating the students for their "inactivity and sleepiness. Why are you such vegetables?"

Peg loved the whole human race - which she felt gave her the right to chastise it when she didn't approve.

The new boy smiled:

"If you could find an old suit for this particular mangy turnip, it might turn into a pumpkin..."

The students laughed, Ed noting that they treated this young man with evident respect: Yu Chi-wei - or David as he preferred to be called - had become an active member of the Communist Party underground while a student at Tsingtao University. Jailed for several months, he was rumored to be the number two man in the CCP in Northern China, living cautiously, never sleeping for more than a few nights in any one house.

He had a girl with him, a young woman: she was skinny with long legs and startling eyes. He introduced her as Lan Ping - Blue Apple.

She was an actress and had been his mistress or "unofficial wife."
She seemed tense, alternately fawning on David and glaring at him:
Ed wondered if she was on drugs, then he remembered the name: ah,
yes, wasn't she the actress who made such a splash in Shanghai
playing Ibsen's Nora in "The Doll's House," interpreting it as a
political rebellion against all authority? "I've been your songbird,
Torvald, a bird trapped in a golden cage..." The Chinese press said:
"this Nora has a Communist's mouth..." It was such a big hit, the
government moved in and closed it down before Ed had a chance to
go and see it himself. Later there was a big scandal when her
husband of the time tried to commit suicide by jumping in the
Whangpoo river...

Perhaps...?

He went over to them:

"Do either of you know a way to get behind Red lines?"

David said nothing; Lan Ping smiled seductively:

"No, but if you find one, let me know, I'll come with you..."

They had to be careful - there were spies all over the campus. But
the Snows had become a safe haven for the students - until, in
December 1936, it became their operations room, and Ed passed his
last test.

Japan announced its intention to set up an independent nation in
Northern China with Peking as its capital.

The students came to Ed and asked him to get a letter to Mme.
Soong asking her advice. Ed came back with her reply:

"Act."

"But what can we do...?"

"The Library and the museums are already packing everything in
crates for the move South..."

"Japanese agents are already opening shops to sell cheap opium
from Manchuria, placing bribes, taking over houses..."

"They've hired troops of professional mourners, pimps and dope
addicts to parade the streets demanding North China's independ-
ence..."

"Chiang?"

"Will capitulate - as usual."

"He has to: the Japanese will declare war otherwise."

"No," said Ed, who'd been up to Manchuria two months ago and knew the Japanese weren't yet ready for full-scale war: "They're bluffing. Stand up to them and they'll back down."

"But how...?"

"Hold a demonstration," said Peg, exasperated by all this shilly-shallying: "stage a mock funeral in the streets: dress up as Japanese and Chinese officials burying the corpse of North China... Show the whole country that the students are ready to stand up and they'll rise up and back you. Use the respect they have for you."

"Yes," said Ed: "We need a demonstration."

"We...?"

Ed blushed:

"I'm as mad as you are," he said: "I'll be there; I'll bring the whole damned Press Corps. I'll film it: the police won't dare stop you then."

That night Ed and Peg translated the students' manifesto into English. The next morning, December 9th, at seven o'clock, Ed's journalism students in the vanguard, eight hundred of them marched into the city through the freezing cold, shouting slogans and carrying banners. Shopkeepers and coolies, monks and merchants stood back and applauded them, then rushed to snatch copies of their leaflets. At a crossroads, a Kuomintang officer got off his bicycle and embraced the students, weeping. But as they neared the Winter Palace, Chinese police reinforced with Japanese gendarmes beat the students with leather belts and tore their banners to shreds, stopping only when they saw the Westerners taking pictures. The students pressed on and at eleven o'clock presented their manifesto to General Ho Ying-chin, Chiang's representative in Peking. It called on Japan to cease its imperialistic moves, and on the Kuomintang to restore civil liberties. Swollen to two thousand, they marched on towards the foreign legation quarter where the fire department turned their hoses on them. But the students seized the hoses and turned them on the police.

Ed filmed it all, conspicuous on the top of Qianmen with his new movie camera, and then rushed back to cable The London Daily Herald:

"Demonstration likely to cause japoprotestupset expected northern settlement stop sinohistory often altered parstudent movement stop student program definitely revolutionary."

The next day, their numbers now swollen to over eight thousand, the students went back, but now the political police, conspicuous in black leather, were waiting for them. They were armed with Mausers, motorcycle sidecars mounted with machineguns, others with fixed bayonets. The confrontation took place in Tienanmen: a tense stand-off, the students defying the fixed bayonets with shouted slogans.

The troops raised their rifles; the foreign press moved forward, cameras ready. And then a small girl rushed out and ran straight at the bayonets; the police grabbed her and began to beat her; Ed rushed over; the police hesitated - long enough for Ed to grab her and take her to safety.

He sheltered her in their house along with other students who'd been beaten, and then got her out of the city.

The news spread fast, the Chinese press translating the Western reports: a nationwide rebellion of youth swept across China, with demonstrations in thirty-two other cities, including Chiang's capital, Nanking.

The Japanese backed down.

"Among all the causes of revolution," Ed wrote: "the total loss of confidence by educated youths in an existing regime is the one indispensable ingredient most often neglected by academic historians."

He was exhilarated - both by the students' courage and his own role. "Now I know why newspaper men in the past got themselves mixed up in China's internal affairs," he said to Peg: "You can't just stand by and watch a lady you love being ravished and do nothing about it. And Peking is a nice old lady indeed."

His part had been noted - by the Japanese secret police, by

Chiang's Blueshirts, and by David Wu. He sat down and wrote a letter to "Mr. K.V.," the code name for Liu Shao-chi. He gave it to one of the many students who had decided the time had come to act and were making their way up to Shensi to join the Reds.

A cave dwelling in Paoan, Shensi province.

Mao is pressing his name-seal on the finished poem, the red square completing the swirling black on white...

His bodyguard enters - accompanied by a young man in a torn blue coat. He bows in awe, holds out a folder in both hands.

Mao takes it, opens it: it is full of press cuttings and a typed, single-page radiogram.

Mao looks up quizzically...

The young man says:

"I think we may have found the man you're looking for...."

PART TWO

HIGH NOON

"Where are the songs of Spring? Ay, where are they?
Think not of them, thou hast thy music too...
The red-breast whistles from a garden-croft;
And gathering swallows twitter in the skies."

Keats,
To Autumn

October 1975, Peking

) Excitement in the air: The People's Daily has just announced a new campaign to "Learn From The Last Seven Years." It's being orchestrated by Jiang Qing's kitchen cabinet: every factory, every Institute, has been instructed to hold weekly public meetings to debate what the Cultural Revolution has achieved so far.

Our meetings are held in the Great Hall of the Institute in which I solemnly take my seat with a virgin pad of paper and three sharpened pencils.

I have been here only once before - for a "Speak Bitterness" meeting: elderly women went up on the stage and spoke about what hunger used to be like, and sickness, how baby sisters were sold, how they scavenged for food in rubbish dumps and loaded frozen corpses onto carts in the winter, tears streaming down their cheeks until people in the audience jumped to their feet and yelled out:

"Never forget Class Bitterness, never forget Class Struggle!"

It all seemed then somehow orchestrated, rehearsed and, this time too, people don't seem to pay much attention, looking out of the window, napping, taking sips of hot water from their thermos flasks. Up on the stage someone reads aloud an article from the People's Daily. When they finish a paragraph, they pause and someone stands up and says: "This is a very important lesson," or "We have been taught a very significant truth here" and then sits back down. My eyes wander. Some of my students are here - one of them already something of a friend, for she's been appointed as our "liaison comrade" - which Ken says means she's a spy. But my wife likes her, and she likes coming to our apartment, where she sits and gazes wistfully at our children. Nobody keeps a child at home; mothers get to see them only on Sundays when, they say, they are very naughty. Yen Wei - or so I shall call her - is sitting three rows ahead of me, on the far left, head down, writing something in a notebook. Her name means Swallow-Tail: it's not her real name, which I'm not going to use for reasons which will become clear as you too get to know her.

She looks up, looks around, sees me staring at her.

Now I haven't come here to stare at women. I'm a married man and if there is a hole in my heart, it's waiting to be filled not by another woman but by an idea - one which will give my life meaning. It happens to all of us, doesn't it: we fall in love with someone, but that then matures into being-in-love: not the same thing. But I think we miss it, retain the memory of that first vertigo, that thrill of falling. And so we look for it, find it if we're lucky - sometimes in another person or in an idea, a vision, one so grandiose, so impossibly idealistic and passionately romantic that it can never be realized. And so never exhausted.

So it was for me; so it was for Ed...

Outside the Hall, I wait for Yen Wei to come out; she sees me, smiles politely, comes over, shakes my hand, says: "We have received your application to go to Yenan."

When I stammer "Yes, but...how...?" she explains:

"I am one of the Worker representatives on the management committee. Have you eaten rice yet, or not?"

So we go together to the staff canteen, a low barn with a bare cement floor and a long trellis-table supporting four huge enamel bathtubs, one full of rice, another of steamed bread and two of stew: cabbage and bean-curd, seaweed and pork fat. All around us people shovel their food down at great speed, dribbling gristle on the floor, which serves also as spittoon and communal handkerchief, for they blow their noses with their fingers and then flick the deposit on the ground.

"There is not a lot to see in Yenan," she says, "and it would be a hard journey for your children. Bei Dai He would be better."

"How do you know?" I ask: "What it's like? Have you been there?"

"Bei Dai He is where all our special guests go in the summer; Chairman Mao himself..."

Yes, I know: he has a villa there, a retirement home, wrote a poem about it:

"Fishing boats on the water

Stretching to infinity

Disappear

But where?"

"No," I say, "I meant Yenan: how do you know there's not a lot to see there?"

"My daughter went there with a Red Guard battalion - in 1968. Even then, it was not the way it used to be..."

"Used to be? You mean you...?"

She looks around, but I am launched:

"Did you meet Ed Snow? What was he really like, is it true he fell in love out there...?"

Her face clouds at the barbarian impoliteness of the directness of my questions.

"You don't know, or you can't tell?"

She shrugs her shoulders, looks round nervously, scowls: "I have to go now," and walks away. I watch her wash her bowl and leave, not looking back, curse myself for being so gauche: how could I ask such personal questions? Haven't you learned anything?

I really want to go to Yenan. My contract entitles me to three weeks holiday a year and it will show good revolutionary consciousness if I elect to go to Yenan instead of the seaside.

But when I ask the Travel Service to book tickets for me, they say there are no trains.

I look at them; they look at me - not impatient, not critical either: impassive.

I have got to know that look - and that there is no point in arguing with it.

Dead end? No: I like to do things for myself, so I go to the railway station. There are guards at the entrance, PLA men - with fixed bayonets. But they see my badge and let me in. In the draughty, cavernous entrance hall, people are sleeping on the floor, using suitcases or bundles of clothes as pillows, children playing hide-and-seek, using their Red Guard armbands as blindfolds. I join the long queue at the ticket counter. But my long nose doesn't entitle me to wait in line like everyone else: they insist I go to the head of the queue:

"I would like four tickets to Yenan, please? Two adults, two children?"

"You have to change at Sian."

"That's all right."

"Soft or hard class?"

"Oh... hard...?"

"Yes, comrade."

Comrade...!

"When for?"

"Next week?"

He told me the date, told me the price, told me the departure time, even the platform number. He apologized that he couldn't actually sell me the tickets. Foreign friends must buy their tickets at the China Travel Service.

"Yes, I know, I just wanted to find out if there were any trains. I will go to the Travel Service now and ask them to phone you: will you set the tickets aside for me?'

"Of course, comrade..."

Outside it was drizzling rain and the sun was setting, but the bus-driver saw my nose coming and here I am now back at the China Travel Service where they're telling me:

"There are no trains to Yenan."

"Would you please call the station? I've just been there myself: they have tickets set aside for me..."

"The phone doesn't work."

The phone isn't listening: it rings. He takes the call, puts the phone down, confronts my raised eyebrow, doesn't even blink:

"It only takes incoming calls..."

Now I've been through all this before. My education began where it should: at a kindergarten. Tracey was placed in a kindergarten - the special one reserved for the children of foreigners, diplomats. We wanted her to go to a Chinese school. After all, she is Chinese.

It was not hard to follow the trail of clicking abacuses and waxy sweet papers left by the children of the Chinese staff - the room attendants who deliver mail, enter without knocking, disturb the papers on my desk, and flick the dust from one corner of the room to the other in accordance with the principle of harassing an enemy you can't wipe out.

Tracey says:

"Why is China so dirty?"

"It's not dirty. It's cleaner than India, isn't it?"

"Yes: it's not filthy, but it is dirty."

"The wind blows dust down from the Northwest. They have planted young trees to stop it, but it takes time. It's not dirt, it's dust."

"Is that why people spit all the time?"

"What?"

"To stop the dust blowing around?"

The children have turned into a gateway, into a dusty yard where a large blackboard covered in pretty chalks tells the children to serve the people and learn from the PLA. Through a grimy window, we watch them sit down at little square desks in a bare room, face front, put their hands behind their backs.

"Is this a Chinese school?"

"Yes, poppy."

"Is that a Chinese lady?"

Pointing with a bent finger:

"Why do the ladies have no hair?"

The teacher is friendly: she pats Tracey's head:

"Of course she can come to school here..."

But when I report this to the hotel management, they look at me impassively:

"There is no kindergarten in the Friendship Guesthouse."

"But it's over there, behind the canteen, by the pond..."

"There is no kindergarten in the Friendship Guesthouse."

On that - first - occasion, I didn't accuse them of lying, of being deceitful: I tried to work out what they really mean, a good reason for their bad answers. What they mean is that my child, like any other child, can't go to any old kindergarten, only the one attached to the place you work. Any other one might as well not exist, their 'non-existence' simply polite shorthand for policy - just as we can't have people wandering around Yenan, the birthplace of the revolution, when we're in the middle of a campaign to radically alter the meaning of that revolution.

So I write a note to the Institute, chaffing at having to do so, feeling a bit like a child constantly asking for toffee apples. This dependence hurts my silly pride: I am used to taking responsibility for my children's schooling, just as I'm used to choosing where to live, what car to buy, what color to paint the walls... Here schools, houses, paint - everything - is attached to a street committee, a commune committee, a factory committee. It is not unusual for an unmarried man to ask his organization to find a wife for him.

I have been here a month now: a fretful period of acclimatization when one confronts the gap between preconceptions and experiences, between the visions and the witness of one's eyes. I have been through this crisis of adaptation before, in other countries, but never like here, where it is aggravated by the artificiality of our lives: half of them spent working with the Chinese, the other living as a Western paterfamilias in a secluded guesthouse. While I am out there, among them, I can turn myself into a butterfly net, catching impressions. But then I come home, the gate clangs shut and I begin to pick over the impressions, hold them up to the light, pull their wings off. It works the other way round too: at home with my books I can go on believing that the ideas are real, the visions true; out there I am faced by the reality of my eyes and have trouble finding the vision.

So we ask to move out. Our apartment costs the Institute 1400 Yuan a month. They could build three houses in a commune for that - even less if they'd let me do it myself.

But they reply that foreigners need central heating, hot running water, carpets on the floor. We protest: that could be considered an insult to my proletarian consciousness.

They say:

"We are pleased that Da Wei wishes to develop a proletarian

consciousness - and that he therefore puts the welfare of others first. If he were to move to a commune, we would have to move many Chinese families out."

I could have insisted; my colleague, Caroline, did: eventually they gave her two rooms in the student dormitory, which meant that eight Chinese students had to go elsewhere. She used to complain that no-one talked to her.

And so it goes on: we would like a cooker in the apartment. After all, it has a kitchen, but:

"They are dangerous for foreigners."

"Sometimes we'd like to eat as a family, not always in the canteen."

"Don't you like the food? Is there something wrong with the food? If there is you should tell the hotel management."

The hotel management provides cars. No-one is allowed to own a private car in China: only cadres have cars - not as a privilege, of course, but because they are very busy. Motorcycles are reserved for the military. The only way to go out as a group is on bicycles - with a sidecar for the children. The police have recently banned children's seats on bicycles, though many Chinese still use them, simply wheeling the bike past the policeman and then cycling on - the only cases of overt civil disobedience I've seen. But some people have sidecars on their bikes: we would like a sidecar for our bikes too, please (it makes me feel greedy, this constant need to ask, and I realize I am slowly building up a childlike gratitude for favors granted, but there is no other way...)

There are no sidecars in the shops; you can't buy the parts either: no Home Depot in Peking. The carpenter at the Guesthouse can't help: he was criticized during the Cultural Revolution for using state tools to make private articles. But rumor has it that, in the industrial city of Tientsin, sixty miles to the South, you can actually buy one!

When we hear of an anti-capitalism exhibition at the Three Stones Factory in Tientsin, we ask permission to go. They have some quite advanced machines for a change and we ask them how they learned to build them

83

"We have no patent rights in China. We freely let foreign countries copy our inventions."

After the tour of the factory and the speeches, we are told we can go sightseeing. Foreigners are a delicacy in Tientsin: out in the street, we attract a crowd of over a hundred and here they don't just stand and stare like in Peking: they jostle for a better view, point and comment. At first we tried to avoid this by dressing in Chinese clothes, anonymous in blue, but we could do nothing about our noses and eyes. I have seen foreigners break down under this constant scrutiny and yell back, which only attracts even more people - who now have something really interesting to stare at.

Our eager chorus follows us from shop to shop. Eventually we get to an alley near the Eastern market where we find several Chinese standing around looking - at three beautiful, homemade, bicycle sidecars! I didn't ask whether it was legal or not, just pointed at one, asked the price: thirty-seven Yuan. We wheeled it triumphantly to the station, followed by a crowd of about four hundred who hadn't had so much fun since the Cultural Revolution.

All we need now is a can of paint...

It wasn't much, I'm not proud of it. A small victory for initiative. But it won't get us to Yenan.

But... it's strange: how victories can sometimes create defeats, and vice versa: a week later, Yen Wei hands me her copy of Ed Snow's story. I'd set it as a translation exercise but instead she's made notes on it, corrections, additions...

How does she know this...?

I

When the invitation arrived, it didn't give him much time to think: "Take the midnight train to Sianfu; go to the resthouse: you will be contacted there by a man who will introduce himself as Wang."

Ed threw things in a bag - the basic necessities of life: Camel cigarettes, Gillette razor blades, a can of Maxwell House coffee... What do you take with you when you're off to interview a man who may have the keys to the future?

Feverish from last-minute inoculations against smallpox, cholera, typhus, typhoid and bubonic plague - endemic in Shensi province, cameras slung round his neck, he took a rickshaw to the train station. Peg went with him, sulking: she desperately wanted to go to Yenan too but they both knew it was impossible and he consoled her as best he could: "Next time...;" "When I get back..."

After she'd waved him goodbye, she went back to the suddenly empty house: "When, or if?"

The train journey took two crawling days: time enough to ponder just who had got him the invitation: Madame Soong, David Yu, or Sergei Polevoy, a Russian émigré Professor at Peking University who Ed had also approached as a potential go-between. Ed would have approached the devil if he thought he knew the way. All he knew was that he was to present his half of a card with English verses on it and match them with someone who would approach him in the hotel. Real Dashiell Hammett stuff: there was also a letter of introduction written in invisible ink, which he was to present to the addressee: Mao Zedong...

As the parched fields drifted past the smeared window, Ed wondered if he had everything he might need: he'd packed a dozen notepads, a clutch of pencils, pens, a pencil sharpener, twenty rolls of film; also diarrhea tablets, Epsom salts, contraceptives...

He rehearsed his questions, jotting down headings on the front page of one of his virginal notepads. The "Celestial Reds" had been isolated by a news blockade for nine years:

Who are your leaders?

What is a soviet?

Who runs the army? What size is it? What are their tactics?

What are these Red theatre companies?

What is "Red culture?"

How do Reds dress, eat, play, make love? Are their women "nationalized?" How does that work?

He planned to be away maybe three months. It was really out of his hands: he was entirely dependent on them when and how he could get back out, but he liked the idea of three months.

He was not to know then that he would want to stay there for good. He was not to know then that his fascination and curiosity, his sympathy and admiration would flare into love. And, in a way, he never did leave there, remaining a captive of that experience until the day he died - the way all great writers become captives of the heroes they create and the myths they weave.

He examined his traveling companions in the dilapidated carriage: a youth and an old man with a wispy gray beard, sipping hot water from a Thermos. The youth was on his way to Szechuan to visit his hometown, though he was afraid bandits might prevent him getting there.

"You mean Reds?" asked Ed.

"Oh, no, although there are Reds in Szechuan, too. No, I mean bandits."

"But aren't the Reds also bandits? The newspapers always call them bandits."

"The editors have to do that: they're ordered to call them that by Nanking. If they called them Communists or revolutionaries, that would prove they were Communists themselves, or sympathetic to them."

"But in Szechuan," Ed pressed him: "don't people fear the Reds as much as the bandits?"

"The rich do, yes, and the landlords, officials, tax collectors. But the peasants don't fear them. In fact they welcome them."

The old man just sat looking out of the window, listening and yet not listening.

"You see," the young man went on, "the peasants are too ignorant. They don't understand that the Reds are only using them - the way they use all people. And they are wicked: they kill too many people."

The graybeard turned his gentle face:

"Sha pu kou!" he said: "They don't kill enough!"

Ed stared at him, flabbergasted by the contrast between his Confucian composure and the violence of his outburst, but then the train pulled into the station, which was crawling with Kuomintang Blueshirts and spies in trilby hats.

Sianfu was occupied by two armies: that of "Pacification Commissioner" General Yang Hu-ch'eng, a former bandit become rich serving Chiang Kai-shek, and the Manchurian army under the "Young Marshal," Chang Hsueh-liang. Driven out of their homeland by the Japanese, for the time being they too chased Reds, though what they really wanted was to go home, drive the Japanese out, not chase fellow patriots around the hills. Although there were 300 Communists in the prisons of Sianfu, thousands were crossing over to the Reds: all this and more Ed found out as he killed time, waiting to be contacted, interviewing General Yang, bemused by his domestic problems. For he was a two-wife man, the first a lily-foot, betrothed to him by his parents, the second a woman he had chosen himself, a former Communist, modern and progressive, who had borne him five children, including three sons. Both wives were refusing to move into his new house unless the other was banned from it. He asked Ed's advice and Ed said: "well, I guess either a divorce or a third wife…" Aside from the symbolism, he didn't really care: Yang to him was typical of the Chinese leaders he already knew only too well: a former peasant who had once dreamed of making big changes in the world but then, finding himself in power, grew weary and confused and settled for mere avarice. Ed felt sympathy neither for his domestic problems nor his migraines and rheumatism: he was going to find an alternative to the whole rotten system.

On the fourth day of fretting and foot-tapping, he found a man waiting for him in the foyer of the hotel. He was large, "somewhat florid and rotund," Ed remembered later: strongly built and dignified, in a long, gray, silk gown. He looked like a prosperous merchant. He got up, put out his hand and introduced himself: "I am Wang Mu-shih, Pastor Wang."

They went to Ed's room and compared cards: the verses fitted! Whose idea was it to choose Keats:

"Season of mists and mellow fruitfulness,

Close bosom-friend of the maturing sun...?"

Perhaps it was Wang - who was totally unexpected. Educated in a missionary school in Shanghai, he'd once had his own church and, like most successful Christians, belonged to the Ch'ing Ping secret society which controlled the traffic in opium, gambling, prostitution and kidnapping - under the protection of the International Settlement authorities. In 1927, it helped Chiang Kai-shek carry out the massacre of the Communists; that was when Wang changed religions and now served Mao as roaming ambassador and go-between. As well as being in Sianfu to welcome Ed and show him the way ahead, he was also reaching a secret understanding with the Young Marshal which would come to a dramatic climax a few months later.

The next day, Wang reappeared in the hotel lobby, accompanied now by a Manchurian army officer, and suggested Ed might like to visit the ruins of the ancient Han city just outside Sian. A curtained car was waiting for them in front of the hotel and when Ed got in, he saw in the back seat a man wearing dark glasses and the uniform of a Kuomintang official. Not speaking, they drove out to the site of the old Han palace and walked over to the raised mound of earth where, two thousand years ago, the Emperor Wu Ti had sat in his throne room and ruled a people he had just successfully united and led out of decades of civil war. Ed picked up some scraps of tile from the old roofs as Wang and the Manchurian officer walked away, leaving him alone with the Kuomintang official.

He walked over to Ed, removed his dark glasses, took off his white hat and grinned mischievously. Ed could now see that he was sun-tanned as no sedentary official would be, and when he came over and took Ed's arm, Ed winced with pain and surprise at the man's strength. He put his face close to Ed's and fixed his sharp, burning, intense eyes on him, all the time holding his two arms in an iron grip. Ed wondered if he'd been set up, but then the man wagged his head and winked!

"Look at me," he whispered: "Don't you recognize me?"

Ed had never met anyone like him in his life. He shook his head apologetically.

The man released his grip and pointed a finger at his nose:

"I thought you might have seen my picture somewhere," he said: "I am Teng Fa. Teng Fa!" he repeated and stood back to see the effect of his bombshell.

Ed knew who Teng Fa was: son of a working-class family, he'd once been a cook on a Hongkong steamer, led the great Hongkong shipping strike, had his ribs broken by a British constable, joined the Red Army and was now the head of its Security Police - with a $50,000 price tag on his head!

Teng danced with pleasure at Ed's amazement and his own audacity: he, the notorious Red bandit chief, living in the very midst of the enemy's camp - disguised in one of their own uniforms! He hugged Ed, said he was overjoyed to see him: did Ed want his horse? What a horse he had, the finest in Red China! Did Ed want to take his picture: he would send instructions to his wife behind the lines to give all his picture collection to Ed, his diary, anything he wanted.

The next day, before dawn, Ed climbed in the back of a Dodge army truck, the wooden gates of Sianfu swung open, noisily dragging their chains, and in the half-light of predawn the truck lumbered out past the airfield where planes were revving up for their daily bombing raid over Red lines. They took the ferry over the Wei River and by noon had reached the city of Ts'un Pu from which Huang Ti, the first Emperor of Ch'in, had supervised the building of the Great Wall.

In the fields, the opium poppies were swollen red, ripe for harvesting.

That night Ed slept in a filthy hut on a clay kang, pigs and donkeys quartered in the next room, and rats in his own. The next morning they entered the strange loess country, that weird, terraced hill-land sculpted of yellow-brown dust blown down from Mongolia, forming a porous but extremely fertile topsoil ten feet deep, constantly replenished and refashioned by the wind. "Scenically," Ed noted in his diary: "the result is an infinite variety of queer, embattled shapes - hills like great castles, like rows of mammoth, rounded scones, like ranges torn by some giant hand, leaving behind the imprint of angry fingers... A world configured by a mad god." There were few houses, the explanation being that the peasants made their homes in those hills too, scooping out elaborate cave dwellings. Cool in summer, warm in winter, they were easy to build and easy to keep clean: even the wealthiest landlords lived in such homes, multi-roomed, with stone floors and high ceilings, lit by rice-paper windows and secured by black-lacquered doors.

At noon they paused at a roadside inn and Ed sat with some Manchurian soldiers returning from the front:

"I bet the Reds eat better than we do," said one.

"Yeah, they eat the flesh of the landlords."

The approach of an officer made them hush: they picked up their rifles and trudged wearily on.

Early in the afternoon of the second day, the truck reached Yenan where the road ended. The walls bristled with machine-gun nests, for the Reds had already begun to make raids this far South and until a few weeks ago had blockaded Yenan completely: hundreds of Kuomintang soldiers had died of starvation and the doors of most shops were still closed and barred. What little food was available was sold to the town by Red peasants who, in exchange for a promise not to attack their Soviet, brought in grain and vegetables.

That night, Ed slipped out of Yenan, crossed the Kuomintang lines and walked the next morning through the no-man's land separating the two armies. Accompanying him was a single muleteer on whose mangy beast Ed piled his bed roll, the little food he'd managed to scrounge and his cameras. There was no road as such, only the bed of a small winding stream running between high walls of rock: the perfect place, Ed realized, for an ambush, a thought not quelled by the muleteer's repeatedly expressed admiration for his cowhide shoes. But then the narrow gorge opened up into a valley green with young wheat and, in the distance, a small cave village. Blue smoke curled from the clay chimneys which poked out from the cliff like fingers:

"Tao-la! We've arrived!"

A young farmer in a turban of white toweling, a revolver strapped to his waist, looked at Ed in astonishment:

"I am an American journalist," said Ed, following the instructions Pastor Wang had given him: "I wish to see the local chief of the Poor People's League."

The man stared and, not taking his eyes off Ed, questioned the muleteer in a dialect Ed could not understand: they seemed to talk for ages, but then the man nodded and said:

"I am that man. I am the chief. Come inside and drink some hot tea."

Ed was eager to move on, but the sun was dead overhead and his host would not hear of him leaving until he'd rested and eaten. Ed paid off his muleteer who turned and trudged back to Yenan: this it is then, thought Ed: I've crossed the Red Rubicon and am now at the mercy of Mr. Dragon Fire - as his host's name translated. He plied Ed with tea, wine, tobacco and questions, soon surrounded by a dozen of his comrades who crowded in to observe the strange foreign devil, examining and commenting on his camera, his woolen socks, the zipper on his khaki shirt. A young woman suddenly appeared, bearing a huge platter of scrambled eggs accompanied by steamed rolls, boiled millet, cabbage and roast pork. The host apologized for the poverty of the meal, Ed for his huge appetite and plunged in the melee of a dozen pairs of snapping chopsticks.

When they'd all burped politely, Ed offered to pay, but Mr.

Dragon Fire indignantly refused:

"You are a foreign guest," he said: "and you have business with Chairman Mao. In any case your money is no good here. Do you have any Soviet money?" and when Ed shook his head, counted out a dollar's worth in soviet paper notes:

"Here, you will need this on the road."

Accompanied by a new muleteer, Ed left the village - not knowing that he was being trailed by bandits, White bandits, in league with the Kuomintang for whom they collected taxes, rents, interest on loans, debts and any other dirty work that needed doing. Later this gave rise to the tale that he'd been kidnapped and killed, for the meal had made it too late for them to reach their intended destination of An Tsai before sunset, besides which his guide's cow had recently calved, there were wolves in the neighborhood and he was anxious to get back to his charges. He deposited Ed in a little village nestling in the curve of a river ten miles from An Tsai. Reassuring slogans decorated its mud-brick walls: "Down with the landlords who eat our flesh!" "Down with the warlords who drink our blood!" but there were no Red soldiers. Ed was offered a bed in the village meeting house, but he declined the foul-smelling room and asked permission to sleep on the two dismantled doors, laying them, Chinese-style, on a pair of benches in the open air where he could gaze up at the stars, and wonder which one was his.

He was roused by someone shaking his shoulder:

"You had better leave a little early. There are bandits nearby and you should get on to An Tsai as quickly as possible."

Swallowing down some hot tea and wheat cakes, Ed set off with another guide along the bed of the stream, passing small cave villages where furry dogs came out to growl at him and child sentinels in red armbands demanded their road pass.

Suddenly they came upon a pool of still water set in a natural hollow basin and there Ed saw his first Red warrior. He was standing by a white pony, which was grazing by the stream, on its back a vivid blue saddle blanket with a yellow star on it. The young man had evidently been bathing and had jumped up quickly when he saw Ed's party approach, pulling on a sky-blue coat and a turban of white toweling - on which was fixed a single red star. He had a Mauser dangling at his hip with a red tassel on the holster. Hand on the gun, he waited for Ed to approach and then demanded his business.

"I have come to interview Mao Zedong," said Ed: "I am told he is at An Tsai. How much further is that please?"

"Chairman Mao is not at An Tsai. Are you alone? I am going to An Tsai: I'll come with you."

Unsure whether he was now a captive or a guest, Ed walked beside the young man for two hours until they entered An Tsai, which they found completely deserted, the whole town nothing but crumbling ruins. The local Red Army detachment had been dispatched to chase White bandits, they were told: they should go on to Pai Chia Ping - which they reached at dusk and where Ed was startled by blood-curdling yells coming from a dozen peasants brandishing spears, pikes and a few rifles.

"Pu p'a," said his guard: "Don't be afraid: there's a Red partisan school here: they are practicing ancient war cries."

Just then a sweating horse raced into the village, and a young commander with a Sam Browne belt jumped to the ground. Looking intently at Ed, he recounted how he'd just returned from an encounter with a hundred White bandits who, the local people said, were led by a really white bandit, a foreign devil!

"We found them about half a mile back," he said, glaring at Ed: "they were following you."

Ed stared at him: was he to find himself now executed as an enemy by the very Reds he'd come to serve?

The tense face-off was interrupted by the approach of a young, slender officer, sporting an unusually heavy black beard. He came over to Ed, the others parting respectfully to let him through:

"Hello," he said: "are you looking for someone?"

Ed suddenly realized the man had spoken in English.

"I am Chou En-Lai, and you are welcome."

And over a meal of boiled chicken, unleavened bread, cabbage, millet and potatoes shared with a dozen young men who taught in the partisan school and operated the clandestine radio, Ed had his first lesson in how to behave in this brave new world. There was nothing to drink but hot water and, though he was parched with thirst, he couldn't bear drinking it. They were being served by two nonchalant young boys in uniforms several sizes too large for them; Ed called to one of them: "Wei, bring me some cold water."

The boy just scowled and ignored him. Ed tried again but with no more success, then saw that one of his tablemates was laughing:

"You can call him 'little devil'," he said, "or comrade, but you cannot call him Wei: there are no servants here."

And at that the cold water arrived.

"Thank you," said Ed: "comrade..."

"Never mind that," the boy replied: "you don't thank a comrade for a thing like that."

Ed knew then that these children, these "red-cheeked little Red devils" were going to be the best thing, the prize, the ultimate proof: "the living spirit of an astonishing crusade of youth."

It was one such kid who escorted him to Chou's office the next morning - a cave dwelling, sparsely furnished, a mosquito net hanging over the kang bed the only observable luxury. Chou was bending over a small desk, reading radiograms; he looked up, smiled, gestured for Ed to sit, handed him a piece of paper. It contained a suggested itinerary for Ed's visit: it would take 92 days!

"This is my recommendation," said Chou: "whether you follow it is your own business. I will give you a horse: you can ride, can't you?"

Ed nodded.

"Excellent. You can reach Pao-an from here in three days: I have sent a radio message ahead: Chairman Mao is expecting you."

And so it was that Ed rode out the next morning, escorted by forty young men. His was the only horse and it was a miserable animal with "a quarter-moon back and a camel gait: his enfeebled legs wobbled so that I expected him at any moment to buckle up and breathe his last." Nevertheless he felt euphoric: everything had been leading him to this point, to this climax - even the horse-riding he'd felt to be such an idle rich man's indulgence back in Peking. Seven years he'd been in China, during which he'd slipped from bemused curiosity through angry frustration to bitter compassion until he desired to play a part in all this, and to hell with journalistic objectivity! What had journalistic objectivity done to stop Hitler who had just seized the Rhineland, or Mussolini seizing Ethiopia? There had to be an alternative, and it had to be out here somewhere, and he was going to find it and report it. For nine years a news blockade had made the Reds more inaccessible than Tibet, but now he, Ed Snow, was riding into Red China, the only Communist-ruled nation outside the USSR, and he would tell its story. Ed had made no agreement or commitment with anyone as to what he would or would not write, but he already knew that it would be upbeat, positive. No-one would be able to check it for years...

It was in such a mood that he entered Pao-An - "Defended Peace" - where what he later described as "a gaunt, Lincolnesque figure with a head of thick black hair grown very long and large searching eyes" came out to meet him.

"I am Chairman Mao," he said.

Two lives had met, joined, drawn to one other by complementary needs and mutual interests.

Well, that's how Ed tells it.

He omits to mention that he was not the only Westerner who crossed the lines that June, that he had not been alone, that there was another American who went with him on that Odyssey, shared what Ed describes as a solitary, epic journey. Perhaps he felt it somehow diminished his own daring and detracted from the uniqueness of his insights to admit that George Hatem had been with him all the way. Or perhaps he didn't want to invite comparison between his own reasons for being there and George's. Hatem was a doctor, one of a close-knit circle of foreign radicals in Shanghai who provided safe houses and communication channels for the Party. He specialized in cleaning up girls from the brothels - until they got the next dose: it was a lucrative business, but when word came down that, as well as an American journalist, the Reds needed a doctor behind the lines, George volunteered. He would devote the next fifty-two years of his life to the Chinese Communist cause and perhaps it was that, his total dedication, that Ed didn't want compared to his own mixed motives. Later Ed would wish he had similarly long-term, useful skills to keep him there too.

And this was not the only thing he forgot to mention when he came to write Red Star Over China.

He doesn't say anything about the girl either. But as he walked forward to shake Mao's hand, one of the young men who had accompanied him to Pao-An hurried across to greet a young woman in a uniform too large her body. Lao Kou had been on the Long March and had been telling Ed about it - and about a girl he had met but then lost after they'd crossed the Grasslands. As he hurried over, the girl looked up and her eyes met Ed's...

Blue Apple

At about the same time Ed crossed over, an actress set out for Yenan on the last leg of her journey towards herself:

"I must find out who's right: the world or me..."

Until then, this had been her finest moment, playing the part of Ibsen's Nora in "The Doll's House:"

"I have only one duty, Torvald: my duty to myself..."

The actor playing Torvald, Zhao Dan, always fell back on a tricky little bit of classical mime at this point in the play: recoiling as if slapped, even touching his cheek to make the point, then turning to the audience, inviting their sympathy. They, Lan Ping knew, would be divided as they always were, every night: shocked that a woman - a wife and mother - could speak like this to a man - her husband and father of their children - but at the same time thrilled by the actress's performance, her passionate identification with the part.

Zhang Min has taught her Stanislavski's method of self-identification, how to draw on her own memories and experiences to feed a character: all the frustrations and humiliations of her own life, all the pent-up venom and unmerited shame pour out of her and carry the audience on a wave of infectious self-assertion, every line in the play a commentary on her own life:

"I've lived by performing tricks for you, Torvald, but that's the way you wanted it. You and Father have done me a great wrong. You've prevented me from becoming a real person."

How much emanated from Nora, the character, and how much from Lan Ping, the actress, is hard to measure. Both Nora and she made exactly the same discovery: the yawning gap between the way they want to believe the world operates and how it actually behaves. Badly. The difference is that, while Nora has only just found this out, Lan Ping has known it since the day she was born, before she became Lan Ping, when she was just little Shumeng ("Pure and Simple"), unwanted child of the concubine of a sixty-year old drunk who beat both the mother and the daughter. It was bad enough that she was a scrawny girl and one born with six toes on one foot; she was also born a rebel, her first act of defiance at four when she ripped off the bandages intended to curb the natural growth of her feet, her second at eight when she leapt at her father who was beating her mother with a spade, got a broken tooth for her heroism but made her mother flee with her, take their chances on the street.

"I must try and educate myself. And I must do it alone."

Mocked by her schoolmates for her cast-off clothes and broken shoes, jeered at as a fatherless child, she was always in trouble at school, beaten and then expelled for daring to fight back. She changed her name to Yunhe ("Crane in the Clouds"), determined to fly, never be trapped.

Then she found the theatre. Here she could enter a world of fantasy, an alternative world, one where justice prevailed and rebellion triumphed, where vengeance flourished and courage was rewarded.

"Now the miracle will happen..."

For she was still naïve enough to think she could transfer all that from the stage into real life, and at first she did: when she was accepted by the Experimental Arts Academy in Shandong on the strength of her long sleek hair, she cut it off. When all the boys chickened out on a dare to steal into the Confucian temple and snatch the ceremonial headdress off the forbidding statue of the stern sage, she did it herself.

"I can no longer be satisfied with what most people say or what they write in books. I must think things out for myself."

Only in one way did she conform to the norms of her time and the traditions of her sex: she saw in men's eyes that her slim, long-legged body was her most important asset, sex the best coin she had to trade. She met, mated and moved in with Yu Qiwei - who liked to be called David and was escaping his own, upper class past by diving into the Communist underground. Basking in the respect and admiration that flowed all around him, she joined the League of Left-wing Theatre People, began to perform in anti-Japanese plays, joined the Party.

The world decided it was time to remind her of the line where theatre stops and reality begins: first David was arrested, imprisoned, hurt. When his family used their connections to get him out, he dropped her, moved to Peking, leaving her to seek consolation in the "bitch-goddess sin-city" of Shanghai. There she discovered women wearing too much make-up, talking back to men, wearing trousers and declaring the entire male sex worthy only of eternal contempt. Yunhe never went that far, but otherwise threw herself into the giddy whirl of street-corner demonstrations, street-theatre agitation, earnest coffeehouse debate and career-building promiscuity. She landed a good role in "The Murder of the Babies" as a harassed working- class woman, and at the end led cast and audience out into the narrow alleys to continue the play in the streets.

"I've discovered that the law is quite different from what I had imagined, and I find it hard to believe it can be right."

Whether Ed ever saw her then I cannot say: they could have

brushed up against one another on their separate ways towards the same star. He could have noticed the striking girl with the long legs and startling eyes on a tram or a bus, or thrusting a leaflet at him, or even when she was arrested one evening in the street by two plain-clothes agents. They answered her question about who is right, the world or her, by dragging her away, stripping her naked and dunking her head in a bucket of water laced with chilli peppers. Then they yanked it out, asked if she was ready to confess yet and when she shook her head, plunged it back under. She tried singing arias from Peking operas in her cell and giving the guards publicity photos of herself to keep her morale up, but she also received gifts of bread and bedclothes, which only proved to her jailors that the Party was looking after her. After four months, her period had stopped, she shook with fever and cold: she could be broken. All they wanted, they said, were some names, a confession - after which they released her into the custody of a foreign YWCA worker.

She was quiet for a while after that.

She called herself Lan Ping now - Blue Apple - and for two months she thrilled Shanghai audiences and herself with her extravagant daring and shameless self-baring:

"Don't you realize you'll be betraying your most sacred duty, your duty to your husband and children?"

"I have another duty just as sacred."

"What's that?"

"My duty to myself."

And then it is over: *"The sound of a door slamming."*

She feels like someone who's lost their shadow - and sometimes like a shadow that's lost its body.

As she sits in the dressing-room taking off her make-up, all she sees ahead of her is a sterile, barren closing-down, drying up: the occasional stage or screen success, the odd scandal, the sex. It all comes to a head when her latest husband tries to commit suicide by throwing himself in the Whangpoo River and she flares for a week or two in the press as a femme fatale.

She sits down then and writes him a letter:

"After going into the theatre, I felt a contradiction, growing sharper each day, between words and deeds. I cannot go on saying one thing and feeling another, pretending to values towards which my heart feels no attachment. I need to take my life back into my own hands. I have glimpsed another life, another world, and now I must make the leap. I cannot help you.

Now I know that, to become who I am, I shall have to change the whole world."

And there is only one place to do that.

She seeks out David in Peking:

"Help me go over. You have the connections, the contacts."

"And what have you got to offer us, to offer them…?"

He pauses, smiles wryly:

"Silly question, I suppose… I can guess what you're thinking, Lan Ping. But listen to me: Mao is twenty years older than you. He has eight children already. And three wives..."

"Yes," she says calmly: "but does he have someone to love?"

There is very little to do in the evenings, on weekends. Wander round the antique shops which are open only to foreigners, looking at calligraphy rubbings, seal-stones, the carved gourds used to keep pet crickets... In a shop near Chien men you can buy the costumes once used in Peking Opera: dazzling, embroidered, silk and satin gowns once worn by Emperors and their concubines. They make great dressing gowns, for Peking Opera is now banned. For the last seven years only eight "model revolutionary works" have been performed, all of them under the guidance and supervision of Mao's wife, Jiang Qing, who has declared the whole repertoire of the classical theatre Confucian, subversive, fit only for the rubbish heap or foreigners: same thing.

It is interesting this: the very real respect for - and fear of - theatre in China.

In began long ago, in the Yuan Dynasty (13th/14th century). The Yuan were Mongols (Genghis and Kublai Khan); after they overran China, they sacked all the Confucian officials who had run the country until then, placing them on the eighth rung of the caste system: one above beggars, but one below prostitutes, who they considered more useful.

Some of them became servants, butchers, wine sellers; others fled to the South and joined the rebels. Most took minor posts in the provinces, wrote poems and waited for the wheel to turn. They did not have long to wait: the Mongols were great warriors, but had little idea how to run a sophisticated nation like China: they found they had to re-employ the despised Confucian scholars, just as Mao did after he took power.

Then as now, they subverted the system from within.

It was not their only strategy: some turned to the stage - as a popular forum on which to keep Confucian values alive. In the first fifty years of the Yuan Dynasty, over 400 plays were written, by over 100 dramatists.

They not only succeeded; they used the theatre as the main

vehicle for a great counter-revolution, a Cultural Revolution: within one generation, the Mongols had become the most ardent, committed, orthodox Confucians China had ever known!

But when they were eventually overthrown - by the Ming, the first thing the new government did was censor the theatre, respecting its subversive power, but fearing it too.

There is nothing like this in Western history, but that is because there is nothing like Chinese acting in the West.

Chinese theatre has always been actor-dominated, not play-dominated: people go to see actors perform, not hear interesting stories told. The plots themselves idealise the Confucian scholar and Confucian values, but the real vehicle of subversion is the actor who, in China, never disappears into a role, but plays it, controls it, shows that we can all perform roles without necessarily ascribing to the values behind them. Chinese theatre is a school of successful hypocrisy which promotes lying and deception as strategic necessities. Chinese heroes happily lie, cheat, pretend, dissimulate; the actors do so brilliantly. And so the fear is obvious: it is that audiences will copy them, learn from the theatre how to survive alien rule by only pretending to believe.

The Cultural Revolution was intended to put an end to that; it came as no surprise to China scholars when it began with an attack on a play, nor that one of the first things Jiang Qing did was ban the whole repertoire.

I am an expert on this. Later I give keynote addresses at international conferences on "The China Syndrome," but now, here, in Peking, though all this helps me understand, it is not especially useful knowledge.

And I have come here to be useful, have I not?

Tell the story, spread the word; even, in my dreams, found a new party.

Because we too could do with a Cultural Revolution, could we not? Why else are people turning so to religion, except for this need to believe, to share a set of values? What are we all waiting for? A sign...?

At the end of one of the most famous of Peking Operas, there is a scene where the heroine, seeking vengeance for her unjust death at the hands of brutal men who punish her for being a good, Confucian wife, prays to Heaven:

"I cry Injustice! Let Earth be moved, let Heaven quake!
Soon my spirit will descend to the deep, all-embracing Palace of Death.
How can Heaven and Earth not make complaint?
Heaven and Earth: it is for you to distinguish between right and wrong,
What confusion makes you mistake a villain for a saint?
The good suffer poverty and want, and their lives are cut short;
The wicked enjoy wealth and honour, and always live long...."

The world is out of joint, and she prays for a sign.

And gets one. Her prayers are answered.

The play is sometimes called "The Injustice Done to Tou Ngo" but it's more popular title tells what happens at the end: "Snow in Midsummer."

II

"Why me? Why invite me? I mean I'm not a Communist - you know that…"

"Precisely because you are not a Communist," answered Mao, pulling voluptuously on one of Ed's Camels: "There is only one way Chiang can stop us now: he can make sure no-one hears about us ever again. A story does not only have to be lived, Mr. Snow, it has to be told. What use is our story if there's no-one to tell it? No-one to believe it? They will believe you because you are not a Communist."

He didn't tell Ed that he also wanted someone who wouldn't know too much about the internal affairs of the Chinese Communist Party. He didn't tell Ed that he needed his help in his ongoing struggles to retain leadership of the Party, to promote and publish his new version of the Marxist message.

"We received a report that you are a reliable journalist, friendly to the Chinese people, and that you can be trusted to tell the truth. This is all we need to know."

Ed nodded: it was a fair deal. If Mao was selective in what he said, if he omitted to mention some things which might tarnish the shiny image, then Ed would meet him half-way: he had no intention of giving any comfort to the enemy by publishing any details they might use against his champion. Such things were irrelevant to his exercise which was, he told himself, to build Mao up, to gain respect for him, and sympathy. If some of that rubbed off on the reporter, well, so much the better. Ed had no intention of going back and saying he'd met a dud, just spent three months with a bunch of losers. Mao was to be presented as the legitimate spokesman of the Chinese masses: "the uncanny degree to which he synthesized and expressed the urgent demands of millions of Chinese." And that was something only he, Ed, was privy to: if you want to know more, folks, stay tuned to this column…

Ed was ambitious, he was a professional, scenting the big story - and how to pitch it, but it was always more than that: he was excited, exhilarated on another level too. He'd come to report on a war of liberation, but what he was finding was not even primarily a war at all, but a revolution. It was intoxicating, this total upside-down-turning of ownership, rights - and from the bottom up this time, boys - and, even more so, girls: radical equality for women too who, as the Man himself put it to him: "hold up half the sky."

"Some of them reckon they've been holding up a lot more than that," the Man went on: "their husbands and sons and fathers all hanging on their back too."

The dead weight of debt, taxes, flood, drought and more debt had, in the case of Chinese women, the additional burden of being tied to a man you never chose, never loved, never had time to get to know. And he no skills of wooing or courting. As single-minded as their donkey. But now: all debts cancelled, along with all titles of owner-ship, mortgages: on the bonfire - along with the marriage certificate too if you want. They were re-inventing themselves out here and Ed was fascinated: compared to this, the rumors that Communist women marched naked and were shared around had no power to move his imagination or his loins. What will such women be like? What would it feel like to be loved by someone like that? How could you feel about someone like that?

It was not a topic on his list of questions and it came as a shock when The Man himself, when Mao brought the subject up.

For a dozen nights, Ed went to Mao's cave with his sharpened pencils and blank notepads, took his place at a small table covered with a red felt cloth and two sputtering candles, placed two packs of Camels on the table and listened as Mao told him his plans, his theories, the precise details of how and why he was going to conquer China. It was fascinating, it was important - it would change the world - but for Ed it was also too abstract, too impersonal. Ed had an item called "Personal History." It included such questions as "How many times have you been married?" When he asked it, however, it came out in Chinese as "How many wives do you have?"

From then on, Ed used the interpreter, painstakingly taking down his translation of Mao's replies word by word and then translating them back, checking them for accuracy. Mao was a night-owl, could speak for hours about armies, tactics, books, connections, resolutions, always fluttering away from the personal. It was partly ideological: Mao didn't consider the individual to be of much importance as a force in history, but it was also tactical: private details could be used to discredit you. There were already enough rumors about Mao's sex-life to fill one of Ed's foolscap notebooks, but it wasn't just sex: Mao was genuinely coy about everything personal, and Ed had to press him hard:

"Enemy propaganda presents you as debauched, ignorant, illiterate bandits, practicing arson, murder, plunder and free love. You've got to counter that - and not just with speeches: you've got to make yourself living persons, not just political slogans. People want to know what sort of a man you are, how you got the way you are. Especially Americans: Americans are interested in people, not in ideas."

Mao laughed: "Not only Americans. I once had a delegation of peasants come to welcome 'Su Wei-ai Hsien-sheng.' They'd heard the new name given to their territory and assumed Mr. Su Wei-ai - 'Mr. Soviet' - was the name of their new conqueror. Lu Hsiang-pang once posted a reward for me in his territory: 'wanted captured, dead or alive, Su Wei-ai."

Eventually Mao relented and told Ed the story of his childhood, his youth, his growing up, how he became a Communist, what it was like in Chingkanshan and on the Long March. Everyone who ever wrote about Mao in the future based their account on what Ed took down in those two weeks. As Mao spoke, he noticed Zizhen hovering in the shadows: much of what her husband was telling Ed she was hearing for the first time too, even though they'd lived together for many years now. Ed thought they seemed comfortable with one another, not showing much of their feelings, she still suffering from the multiple wounds of a shrapnel bomb which had burst and spat splinters of metal into her tough little body. There were only two rooms in the cave, the walls decorated with maps: it lacked any real privacy, the only moments of domesticity when she interrupted them with food, especially Mao's favorite: bread baked with red hot peppers. But even that Mao could turn into a theory:

"Have you noticed, Mr. Snow, that you find revolutionaries only in countries where they eat lots of red peppers? No, look: Spain, Mexico, Russia, France..."

He ticked them off in between mouthfuls of hot bread:

"And here, in China: Hunan, Szechuan..." and then launched into a rendition of "The Hot Red Pepper Song" which tells how the pepper, disgusted with his pointless vegetable existence waiting only to be eaten, leads the cabbages, spinach and beans in a great insurrection.

Zizhen smiled but she'd heard it before, and retired as if to nurse some private sadness: Ed knew they'd left their two children behind in Kiangsi at the very beginning of the Long March and now they could not be found. Before Ed left Red China, Zizhen would present Mao with a baby girl, but by then it would be too late...

It could have been that evening, after she'd gone to bed, leaving the two men alone, that Mao got up from the stool at the table, stretched, sat down cross-legged on the kang, leaned back against his dispatch boxes, lit a cigarette from a candle and said:

"Have you, Mr. Snow, ever experienced romantic love?"

Ed wasn't sure he'd heard right: Mao had a soft, Southern accent which spread the vowels and slurred the consonants, but the Man went on:

"I have read of this in translations of your poets Byron, Shelley, Keats. Have you ever known love such as this?"

Years later, on her death-bed, Ed learned that Mao had asked the same question of Agnes Smedley, when she'd followed Ed to Yenan:

"I was amazed at his childlike curiosity," she recalled: "He told me he often wondered whether the kind of love he had read about in Western poetry and novels really existed. And what it would be like."

Evidently he'd never felt it himself, or he wouldn't have needed to ask the question; Smedley said he even admitted as much and that "he seemed to feel like he'd been cheated somehow."

Ed wasn't sure that Agnes Smedley knew much about it herself. He didn't tell her that while he was there, in Pao-an, he was pretty sure that Mao was still hoping for it, looking for it, the elusive "wild ecstasy." Not in his wife, nor in her predecessor, his child-bride; in ideas, of course, in visions, in Utopias certainly, but hoping still that he might also find it one day in a pair of eyes. These were Romantic times - not yet the cold cruelties of cementing power or the crude realities of revenge, Mao not yet the distant Buddha on the dais. The Man was energetically, magnetically alive. No arid intellectual this: a man of the soil as much as the library, a man who lived in his body as much as in his head. Thick, blue-black hair worn long, searching eyes glinting, wide, thick lips: Ed loved to watch him in the audience of the plays they sometimes put on in the village square. Mao would sit there, imitating the gestures of the actors, pursing his lips when they roared with anger, waving his arms when the firecrackers exploded, and glowing with a wild joy when an army of stage peasants in embroidered costumes finally overthrew their feudal lord. The Mao Ed got to know understood passion. When he wrote one of his famous articles, he didn't sleep for days, sitting, socks round his ankles, frayed cuffs unbuttoned, spare hand reaching down to scratch for fleas in his baggy trousers, utterly absorbed, overlooking his meals, his only refreshment an occasional mop of the face with a hot flannel. His bodyguard told Ed that, until Mao finished "On Practice," he wouldn't eat - for seven, eight days, getting perceptibly thinner, eyes shot with blood, so engrossed he didn't even notice that a fire was burning a hole in his right shoe until he jumped up in pain: "How did that happen?"

Ed had a fuzzy realization that all this was perhaps a substitution thing: that the love of ideas, the passion for Utopias were a substitute for a woman. He understood, therefore, why the subject of Romantic love should interest Mao, why the question of its existence should bother him. But at that time Ed didn't have an answer for him:

"I'm not sure I've ever felt it... Which I guess means no. If I'd felt it, I guess I'd know it..."

Wouldn't I?

Ed had never fallen in love. He'd been loved, but that is really very different. Which is why, when it happened, he was unprepared: a foreigner in a strange land.

Until then, he'd known love only as the feeling you get after someone falls in love with you. That nurse in Burma, Peg... When he met someone like that, someone he liked, he wanted her to love him, to be his, so that when he had doubts about himself, she would be there, the eyes would be there. Bright mirrors. Love made him feel good about himself, affirmed him, gave a cocky lift to his walk.

He thought that was all you needed to know on the subject.

In this respect he was very much like Mao - which is perhaps why they tended to like the same women: they went to women to be loved by them and they loved them back, but it was always a secondary response - a kind of gratitude, a form of narcissism. If you'd asked Ed, he would have said: all I want is to love and be loved - not realizing that they are two quite different emotions, sometimes mutually exclusive, even incompatible. Falling in love doesn't calm doubts, it aggravates them; it doesn't affirm, it questions; it is all giving and wanting. It can hurt.

Ed doesn't say how or even whether he answered Mao's question about Romantic love. Byron, Shelley and Keats were not poets he knew well; indeed, the whole territory was about as foreign to him as ancient Greek. That changed - for both of them: though they never got to talk about it, they both learned about it and at about the same time.

It was Mao who provided the introduction for Ed. One evening, towards the end of his two weeks of interviews, Mao's bodyguard came in and whispered in Mao's ear. Mao nodded, said: "Send her in."

She was still wearing the same oversized uniform. So did a lot of the child-soldiers, and many of them wore their hair short too - in a kind of swallow-tail at the nape of the neck. But as the girl stepped through the cave door, the flickering candle light made a Cubist painting of the planes of her face, the high cheek bones, hollow eyes, proud jaw and sharply defined lips. Ed just stared.

He both knew her instantly, recognized her, and yet had never seen anyone like this ever before.

Mao took the papers she held out to him and, as he read them, Ed's eyes wandered wonderingly all over the girl's face, turning away only when she glared at him in angry embarrassment, but then watching her out of the corner of his eye, soaking her in.

He heard Mao's voice asking:

"Where is he now? General Chu?"

She looked across at Ed, frowning, but Mao smiled:

"You can speak in front of Uncle."

"About a hundred Li South-West of here..."

Mao nodded, turned to Ed: "I must unfortunately interrupt our discussion; I must work tonight..." He turned to the girl: "Come back at midnight; I will have papers for you to take back."

And then, as Ed rose to his feet and gathered his papers, Mao added:

"Oh, you should ask this girl to tell you her story. You said you wanted a human interest story..."

And when the girl frowned fierce eyebrows and shook her head vehemently, Mao added softly:

"There is more than one way to serve the Party, little one..."

He smiled his Buddha-smile:

"Mr. Snow is a friend of the Chinese people. He has our permission to go wherever he chooses, talk with whomever he likes. He has come to tell our story, tell the truth about us. You can trust him."

The girl lowered her head, muttered almost inaudibly "I'm sorry, forgive me," blushed, scowled, turned and fled.

Now it must be said that Ed had a perfectly respectable, professional interest in this girl: from the brief words she'd exchanged with Mao he'd gathered that she brought messages from Chu Teh. He had already noted that Chu Teh was not in Pao-an: instead of his presence, there were rumors about his absence - that he'd fallen out with Mao, that he resented playing second fiddle to him, that Chang Kuo-tao had kidnapped him and was holding him as hostage and potential ally in his ongoing struggle with Mao for supreme leadership. No-one denied that the army had split in two before crossing the Grasslands and that Chu Teh was now leading the other half in.

The girl might know something, and the Man had said he could go anywhere, ask any questions...

But when he walked out into the warm embrace of night, she was nowhere to be seen.

No: she's going to wait until he's passed, until he's disappeared behind a door, until it's shut firmly behind him, until the lights go out, then she'll come out from the shadows. If necessary, she'll even go to the Fraternization meeting at the Lenin Club, as Lao Kou said she should, though she doesn't want to go, hates them. If she wears her hair short it's not because she's a modern Shanghai girl aping Mae West; it had been shaved off - by the Kuomintang when they took her in for questioning. They did other things to her too, and after they threw her out in the street, naked, wet with pepper water, sperm and sweat, she had kept her hair short all the way to Chingkanshan and then all the way through Tibet and across the Grasslands. But now the order has gone out to persuade as many Kuomintang soldiers as possible to come over to the Red side, promise them they can then get to fight the real enemy, the Japs, tell them that in the Red Army they won't be beaten, that over here officers go in ahead of the men, not behind them. She hates these fraternization meetings: the sly bastards always ask about ransom money, about loot, booty, women; they're told firmly none of that: if you want that, go back to the other side and one day we will come and shoot you. Because that's the best reason to come over to us: we're going to win.

She understands the need for such meetings, for such a policy, but she still hates them: the soldiers' eyes running over her body: she knows what they want. But she has to smile at them, persuade them, invite them over.

And now there is this long nose with the round eyes, staring at her shamelessly, and Mao says she is to talk to him if he wants.

She intends to avoid both the meeting and the impertinent foreign lecher by loitering in the shadows outside Mao's cave: if anyone sees her, she can always say she's waiting for an urgent dispatch to take back to Chu Teh...

Ed's torch sweeps the empty square: he doesn't have many batteries left but is sure this is worth it: yes, there she is, hiding - as he guessed she would be, the timid little wild thing. But he's got her trapped in the beam and walks across to her now, smiling, hand out:

"Hi, I'm Ed Snow, do you want a cigarette?"

His Chinese is not so good, but good enough: she understands him, Mr. White Cloud, with his pack of Camels to tempt her, buy her, carry her away.

She shakes her head. She really doesn't want this: hers is not a story you tell to a stranger. Not to anyone. Not even yourself. The shame is too great to bear.

He is lighting a cigarette; in the flash of the match, she notices that his eyes are blue; he's saying:

"Chairman Mao is very kind, but you don't have to tell me anything - unless you want to? Are you sure you don't smoke?"

"I have a meeting to attend..."

"May I come with you? I want to tell the world the truth about China, about you. The best way to do that is to collect stories, personal stories, let them speak for you. Did you know that your General Chu Teh, when he was very small, was given away to his parents' relatives? That they drowned five other children? A detail like that: it sticks in the mind..."

He laughs; she notices that he has dimples under the red stubble.

"They also say that when he joined Chairman Mao in Chingkanshan, they captured his wife, cut her stomach open, sliced off her breasts and then tossed the body back over the line. I think I'd go mad if that happened to me, but details like that are worth more than a thousand speeches."

Ed too felt awkward. He didn't know the rules out here. How do you address, what do you say to a girl who's wearing an old, faded, patched, green cotton soldier's uniform, a battered peaked cap with a red star on it, a holster with a gun, and a dagger in her belt? A girl who has the wary suspicion of a wounded forest animal in her eyes, and a deep silence within as if she carries an urn...?

He didn't find out, not that evening: someone else was looking for her that evening and now found her: Lao Kou, the young man Ed had befriended on the way here, suddenly appeared out of the dark night, went over to the girl, smiled at her, said "The meeting has started already," then turned to Ed:

"This is the girl I was telling you about. We are going to be married."

The girl looked down at her feet scuffing the dust, flicked her eyes up at Ed for just an instant, turned and strode away, swallow tails flapping.

Ed was an insomniac. They'd housed him in the "Foreign Office" - four one-room mud-brick huts - as a guest of the Soviet state. He couldn't easily go out at night for fear of arousing suspicion: there were some around here who were sure he was really a spy. So he just lay there, tossing and turning fitfully: that was when the girl came to him, very vividly, her face looming out of the cave of his memory, blending and merging with other faces that haunted him, whose eyes would not let him go... She was everything he couldn't be: isn't that love, Romantic love: when you meet your missing half?

An Apple For Teacher:

Lan Ping had been in love before. She'd slept with men too, but some of them she'd fallen in love with.

They all hurt her, used her, and she moved on.

But she hadn't yet reached the stage where there is only calculation and no passion, and hopes she never will. Being in love feels better than not being in love: she just needs to find someone who is her equal, someone who won't let her down. They have been too ordinary, the men in her life; they were not complex enough. She knows she can make someone a strong, rich, complex other half. She just hasn't met him yet, that's all.

It hadn't been so hard after all to go over to the Reds: after the student uprising in Peking, many people went across - students mostly but also accountants, blacksmiths, printers, writers, actresses.

She crossed over in Sian. The small town they sent her to for training was dusty, drab, hot: chickens and donkeys in the street, a muddy river. The men wore towels round their heads and sunglasses hiding their eyes.

She was accepted into Party School - one of only ten women among three hundred students: classes are held in the former Catholic Church, where they're taught their Engels, their Maoism, military tactics. The women, she notes, deliberately neglect their appearance, wearing their uniforms shapelessly and their hair brutally short - as if femininity is a sign of weakness. Lan Ping knows better, nipping the baggy gray uniform in tight at the waist and then tying the belt with a bold bow, her hair worn long in two braids decked out with blue ribbons. The training is hard - learning how to fire a gun, throw a grenade, how to live with diarrhea and cold. One day she goes up to the pagoda on the hill and looks down on the little town: she'll ask to be transferred to an opera troupe: all the Party bosses are opera fans.

And now he's here! The students have been summoned to a special talk by a "leading comrade." Lan Ping has spent extra time on her hair and arranging a bright orange scarf round her neck and now she's late: his car is already there, drawn up outside the old Church. Everyone knows this car: it has an inscription on the side: "Ambulance Donated by the New York Chinese Laundrymen's National Salvation Association."

But her friend Xu has saved her a stool in the font row; waiting for the leading comrade to enter, Lan Ping tunes up by joining in the singing. Her trained voice rises above the others - and then continues on, just for a moment, after Mao comes on stage. The whole audience stands and claps; Lan Ping claps just a little bit longer than anyone else. He looks at her. He isn't so old, she thinks: mature, experienced, sure of himself, vigorous. But not complete, not self-sufficient: what man is? She's already heard the rumors about his marriage breaking up - his wife worn out, her body wrecked from shrapnel and producing five children in seven years. They say her mind wanders, that she's being sent away for treatment. Some say to Moscow: everyone knows what that means...

After the speech is over, waiting for him to come out and get in his car, Lan Ping says to Xu:

"He looks lonely, don't you think he looks lonely?"

She snorts: "Lonely? They say he's learning to dance; that there are dances being held in some of the leaders' caves. They say he's found a new love: Lily Wu..."

"Lily Wu?" cries Lan Ping, who knows the woman: from Shanghai: a poet, divorcee and actress: "What's she doing here?"

"She came with an American woman. Agnes Smedley. She is her secretary, her interpreter. They say he writes her poems."

Lan Ping is not too worried by this news: she wants Mao unencumbered by any wife, but she knows enough about how things are organized around here to know that the woman who takes Mao away from Zizhen will not be the one allowed to take him over. Marriage breakers become past lovers, not future wives.

That was a month ago; tonight he's coming to see her again and, this time, see her where she belongs: on a stage. She knows he loves the theatre and has chosen her part carefully. She has the rest of her life to play the Emperor's Concubine, and everyone loves "The Fishermen's Daughter." Based on a chapter in his favorite outlaw classic, "The Water Margin," the play celebrates the rebellion of a bandit turned fisherman against a landlord:

"At last you've returned, Father. But why are you in such a dreadful state? You have been most barbarously treated..."

"Fetch me my coat and cap and my steel sword."

"I'll come with you, Father."

"You are a girl: you had better stay at home."
"But isn't this a fine chance to show my courage?"
"All right: come along then."

There are good arias in "The Fisherman's Daughter" but what everyone loves are the mime scenes, especially those where the girl pretends to be rowing and then balances precariously on a rocking boat. A good actress extends these sections as long as she feels the audience can be held by them. As Lan Ping minces her way out on stage, her eyes scan the audience: there he is, with his long, sleek hair and wide, thick lips.

She begins the scene: she has every intention of stretching it as far as possible.

She may totter and she may teeter, but Lan Ping has every intention of falling.

Our apartment has become popular with the African students who've come here to study guerrilla warfare. They like our records, and the opportunity to dance with a woman. Though officially welcomed and cherished as special friends of China who will one day spread the Chinese version of Marxism to a whole new continent, the average Chinese fears and despises them for their colour.

They are constantly complaining about this, especially about their inability to meet, let alone date a Chinese girl.

There are rumours that Elizabeth puts out for them: sex is a major topic of gossip in the Friendship Guesthouse, though Ken, who's been here the longest, says that sex in China has become very simple: a zero - without the line round it. Others say sex has become what it is: a natural function with a social purpose: to have children. Every commune, every street committee has a Birth Allocation Chart, noting which woman has earned the right to have the next child. Every commune and street committee has its own crèche and its own kindergarten too: 80% of the women work, one salary being enough for two people but not for more, so the paradox is: you can stay at home if you don't have children, but not if you do. Not to go out to work is, however, shameful, for it means you have a bourgeois husband who keeps you at home for his own private pleasure, which is disgusting.

Ken scoffs at all this, says China is turning into a nation of great masturbators and underground homosexuals. I have yet to see a boy hold hands with a girl in the street or the park. There is a great deal of back-stroking, thigh-patting and hair-petting but only among members of the same sex. Only once have I seen girls dressed differently from boys - on October 1st, which is Bastille Day, July 4th, V.E. Day and Harvest Festival all rolled into one. In all the parks, workers festoon the trees and bushes with crepe paper flowers, butterflies, birds and bees. Painted pansy faces are pinned on the weeds. From some central nursery, pots of real dahlias, chrysanthemum and salvia have also been trucked to the parks, flowers otherwise forbidden as bourgeois.

Girls are lined up in ranks at the entrances: they have skirts on and bob and twist through the simple steps of a welcoming dance. Boys gaze at them in bewilderment, shocked by this sudden transformation of so many baggy-trousered, severely coiffed mini-amazons into sylphs wearing lipstick and powder and showing off their knees. They are as delicately pretty and pert as anything in Hong Kong or Singapore, peering with coyly tempting eyes over paper fans. Where did they learn to hunch their shoulders like that, where did they learn the throwaway lingering glance back over the shoulder? No wonder this is allowed only once a year... It is all very demure, but the total absence of advertising sirens, movie posters and newspaper pinups makes even a bare knee a revelation.

When I try talking about this in class, everyone becomes very coy. Yin Wei alone has an opinion - but one she will confide only in the privacy of a park:

"We Chinese have long been objects of Western sexual fantasies," she says: "You have always had this image of Chinese woman as... 'compliant:' is that the right word? You have seen our pillow books and know that Chinese women are able to bend into positions very hard for Western women but pleasing to Western men. We are supposed to have no shame, inexhaustible, always ready, will do anything you ask.

You could not be more wrong: Chinese women have always been treated by our own men as sex objects. And so we have no real interest in sex at all.

You have spoiled it too much for us."

"And love?" I ask.

"Ah," she smiles down at her reflection in the river: "That is different. Sometimes I think it is better without sex.

That way it lasts.

Perhaps for ever..."

III

It hurt him to look at her.

To want something so badly - and know it can never be yours.

But he still went looking.

Ed had dated girls before, but on August 15th 1936 he knew that everything he'd ever learned about how to approach a woman who catches your eye was irrelevant, useless.

Invite her to what movie, to what party, dinner for two in which cozy restaurant?

There isn't even a teahouse...

He might as well be on the moon.

How do you court a moonbeam?

He stood in the pale morning sun in the dusty street, rubbing his eyes, tired from chasing her all night through the draughty caverns of his mind. He felt timid, insecure, willing her to appear and yet fearful of her eyes. Peasants with braided hair wrapped round their heads were herding shaggy goats, women in white turbans wheeled barrows of dew-studded melons while little Red Devils in skeweyed caps carried water to make morning tea and swept the road outside their barracks with a broom of millet stalks. In the distance someone was practicing bugle calls, a courier on a sweating horse galloped past, a man in a white skullcap led his camel down to the river, and the breeze flapped the corner of a poster on a mudbrick wall: "Every enemy soldier who comes over is worth double: he does not shoot at you; he shoots with you." Perhaps he should have gone along to that Fraternisation meeting last night, after all...? No: the thought of her smiling seductively at some leering, pockfaced butcher made him shudder.

How do they reward those who come over?

Do you get to stay the night?

I've come over...

Not for the first time, Ed wondered whether the overt Puritanism of this army of virgin soldiers simply reflected the lopsided ratio of women to men or whether it concealed a very active underground sex scene. There were rumors - of dances in leaders' caves, of Shanghai actresses, poker games... But all the women he saw were shapeless - and deliberately so, it seemed, almost arrogantly. Well, they held all the trump cards, didn't they. All across the mountains and the grasslands, their scarcity had been such that they'd never had to care about their appearance, the shy local women never a threat, barely a temptation, the traditional privilege of rape forbidden. Ed sensed that this would change as city girls began to come across but he didn't care about them, about anyone else: where was she?

He scratched his chin, suddenly embarrassed by the ten-day ragged stubble, by his stinking armpits, foul breath and dusty, tangled hair...

And then Lao Kou appeared from the barracks, buttoning up his jacket.

Ed said - casually, he hoped, off-hand:

"How was the meeting last night?"

Lao Kou frowned: the word Ed had used for meeting - "huan-hui" - could have all sorts of connotations - assignation, rendezvous - some of them covered by what the long nose said next:

"She's very nice - your fiancée."

Lao Kou just blushed, but Ed was launched:

"How old is she? Where is she from? When do you expect to get married?"

It was all much too personal, much too direct: you don't talk like that around here. But Ed was excused in advance, almost expected to be gauche, to be rude, to behave like a barbarian. With him there were no rules. In any case, Lao Kou already knew that Ed wanted the girl's story - she'd told him so - and so he was bound to find out eventually:

"First she must have tests."

"Tests?"

"To see if she can have babies. We want to have babies, but..."

Ed had a way of encouraging people to trust him, open up to him. And anyway, over here there is no more shame:

"She had an abortion. Three years ago. It is not sure she can still... You know..."

"Oh, I'm sorry," Ed heard himself saying as his mind pounced on this sudden piece of information, trying to gauge what it meant. For them, for him, for her... But even as his brain explored this tidbit, turning it this way and that, he heard himself adding:

"Is there anything I...?"

"Can you tell your government to send us medicines? Planes too, of course, and machinery, but especially medicines?"

"I don't know anyone in the government."

"But America is a democracy - or not? The government serves the people, or not?"

"It's... more complicated than that. What medicines do you need?"

"Penicillin. Quinine. I'll make you a list."

"Yes. Good. Thank you."

"Is there anything I can do for you?"

Ed stared at the boy: yes, of course, everything, though nothing he could ask:

"Do you think...? If she'd tell me her story... How she came to be here..."

"It is perhaps not so interesting. Chairman Mao..."

"Has given me permission."

"I can ask her for you."

Yes, good, thank you.

I won't hold my breath...

The problem was that Ed was due to leave, any day now - for the long-awaited dream-visit to the front line. It had once been his greatest ambition, this first-hand look at the Reds in action. Yes and now: not only see them in action, but ride out there with a woman who is also a revolutionary - that would be something! And he did have one useful piece of new information: Lao Kou had said he'd ask her, therefore she must still be here...

He tried the tennis courts: love-fifteen; the basketball court: time out. The University? He'd promised to give a talk there before he left. It occupied some bombproof caves which had once served as storerooms for landlords to hoard grain and treasure. For chairs, they used a pile of bricks, and for paper the back side of enemy propaganda leaflets. Its President, Lin Piao, had given Ed a blanket invitation to speak to the students: he'd give a brilliant speech and afterwards she'd come up and ask him to help her with her essay...

But as he surveyed the class, he counted only ten women among the three hundred men, and all of them determined to expose him as a sham with their sharp questions:

"Why has the League of Nations failed?"

"Why is it that, although the Communist Party is legal in America, there is no workers' government in your country?"

"What is the significance of Leith-Ross's visit to Japan?"

Afterwards they wanted to go on asking him more and more questions to which he had less and less answers. Only one of the women smiled at him, but it wasn't her smile. It didn't matter: Ed had never been any good at flirting with the well-bred young ladies he'd taught in Peking, and at least there he could offer to wheel their bike or lend them a book...

She wasn't in the canteen at lunchtime; she wasn't in the Lenin Club where he wasted the whole afternoon reading the wall newspaper, and the little Red Devils lined up to take turns thrashing him at ping-pong.

Then he remembered: it was Saturday: she was bound to be at the theatre - it was such an occasion, a theatre performance: everyone went.

Ed took up his position two hours before sunset, occupying a crumbling wall overlooking the open-air stage in the old temple down by the river. It gave him an excellent view of the audience. He watched them wander down - soldiers but also muleteers, carpenters, clerks from the co-op and the postoffice, women from the shoe-factory with their children. No tickets were sold; people just sat on the grass. He saw Mao wander down with a woman he'd been told was a poet from Shanghai called Ting Ling and take his seat next to a family of local peasants, Lin Piao in among the students. She still hadn't shown up by the time they whisked open the makeshift, pink silk curtain. He sighed: Ed had never liked Chinese theatre, the falsetto singing and clashing cymbals of classical opera, but was rather enjoying the slapstick of this show, its robust vitality and earthy humor - when he suddenly realized that they were all looking at him! There had been a short play called "Invasion," in which grotesque caricatures of Japanese soldiers used Chinese men as chairs, made drunken love to their wives, forced peasants to buy opium, entered a village market place, demanding identification papers, stealing food, shooting anyone who resisted. It ended with everyone rising up to butcher the Japanese pygmies, but then members of the audience stood up too and, voices shaking with emotion, cried out "Death to the Japanese bandits!" Then a group of a dozen girls came on, barefoot, in peasant trousers and coats and fancy vests, silk bandannas on their heads, first performing a folk dance and then something called "Dance of the Red Machines" in which they interlocked arms, legs and heads and imitated the turning of cogs and wheels, the hum of dynamos, the thrust and drive of pistons. While Ed was still recovering from that, someone sang a local folk song, followed by a command performance by a youth who played good harmonica and then, to Ed's utter consternation, a demand that the "wai-kuo hsin-wen chi-che" - the foreigner newspaperman - sing a solo for them! And he'd just seen her...! Walking down... Alone...!

He stood up, hoping she'd see him. See him? Everyone was staring at him, already smiling in anticipation:

"I could think of nothing but fox trots, waltzes, La Bohème, and Ave Maria," Ed wrote in his diary that night: "which all seemed inappropriate for this martial audience. I could not even remember The Marseillaise. The demand persisted. In extreme embarrassment I at last rendered The Man on the Flying Trapeze. They were very polite about it. No encore was requested."

And all the while the girl watched.

Well, I can't make more of a fool of myself than that, Ed told himself. I'll just go and ask for her. After all, they said they'd give me whatever I need...

He made it up as he went along: he'd need a guide when he went to the front, someone reliable, someone he could talk to, someone whose story he could tell, a companion...

They said nothing, just sat and looked back at him, not impatient, not critical either: impassive. Ed liked to think he'd got to understand the Chinese; they never made that mistake: a barbarian is always a barbarian: what is this he wants?

"Perhaps I could go and see Chu Teh...?"

"Too far."

"Then someone who was on the Long March with him?"

Ah...

"Like that girl...?"

Ah...

"That courier...?"

Ah, yes.

"Chairman Mao said she was to tell me her story... We could do it on the way to the front..."

They didn't like it. He could tell from the way they looked back at him as he stumbled his way along that they didn't like it.

But he was their guest and there was so little they could offer him in the way of hospitality or recreation. In the society they came from, a foreign guest of importance would be taken to the opera, to dinner, even to a dance hall if he was that way inclined...

They turned and spoke to each other: Ed couldn't follow it all, but it was about Mao, about enemy propaganda, about the need for friends... and he suddenly understood: they were getting to it their way, trying to find a good reason to agree to his bad request. Because it was bad, he knew it was bad: to ask for a guide, even a girl is one thing; to specify a particular one, an individual, betrayed bad bourgeois consciousness. Ed didn't care: they could get to it any way they liked.

He wasn't there when they told her. She bit her bottom lip and said she didn't want to go. They told her it was their wish. She was just a girl in a shapeless uniform for whom they had a part. They were still struggling their way out of the old and she was still stuck in it, deep down, inside: she obeyed.

And so when Ed opened the door of the Foreign Office the next morning and stepped out for his morning smoke, he found not one horse but two waiting for him, and on the second a scowling girl.

He nodded at her, smiled, looked away before the scowl made him blush and regret what he'd done, ground out his cigarette, ran in, got the bag he kept permanently packed and his camera and didn't care that there was also an escort of six cadets riding with them. He expected some resentment, but was confident that in a few days he could thaw the chill. It didn't bother him that conversation was at first desultory, full of "Excuse me's" and "I don't understand's:" the presence of her on the horse next to him, the fact of her, the physical fact of her thigh against the horse's flank, her buttocks bouncing on the hard wooden saddle, the small of her back, the nape of her neck, even the pursed, stubborn lips and aggressively jutting jaw: it was enough.

They stopped at noon by a cool stream in the shade of a small orchard of wild apricots. The boys stripped off their trousers and shirts and jumped in, then lay down on a long flat rock in the shallows, the water rippling over them like a cool sheet. She sat apart, declined Ed's offer of a cup of coffee - the most precious gift he had. But she did take the camera when he showed it to her, did point it at things and when he asked her to take his picture, she did turn it on him and he could look straight at her and grin and stare and hope he didn't show too much. Or too little.

As they rode through a landscape of bald sloping hills, patch-worked with fields of millet, cotton, cabbage and melon, he fed himself on all her little mannerisms, her little tics, the things that made her special, unique: the way she flicked her plaits, the two deep furrows like trenches between her eyes when she frowned; the dimple that hollowed her cheek when she tried to look cross; the way she slipped her feet out of the stirrups and let them swing free...

That night they stopped in a village where the headman showed them their quarters and which ovens they could use. Two local women volunteered to pull the bellows for them and then stayed behind to joke with the boys. They were a mixed bunch - from Szechuan, Fukien, Shensi, Kansu: one escaped slave, two deserters, the rest volunteers who had joined when their parents were killed in a bombing raid, their sister abducted: the usual cruelties. There was a remarkable easiness about the way they mixed with the local peasants: they all seemed to have a positive attitude about life, almost, Ed thought, a kind of happiness - so different from the passive contentment which was the best most Chinese he'd met ever showed or ever hoped for. They were aged between seventeen and twenty-four and:

"I often have a queer feeling among the Reds that I am in the midst of a host of schoolboys, engaged in a life of violence because some strange design of history has made this seem infinitely more important to them than football games, textbooks, love, or the other main concerns of youth in other countries."

But they had none of the impatience of youth. This was a war of attrition and it would take time for the enemy to be worn down, their resistance broken. Ed didn't have the time for long sieges, ambushes, decoys, diversions, all the strategies of a guerrilla campaign. As a boy took up a guitar and sang softly into the night, he fell unhappily off to sleep.

Then she came to him, down by the river, undressing, slipping into the water. Her body in the moonlight was hairless; cream skin like a peeled peach. He gasped at the sight of her small, firm breasts pouting as she raised her hands and ran them through her sleek, black, wet hair, and then turned, smiled at him.

The next day, head still seething with these siren images, he tried discussing Marxism with her:

"What you have here is really only equalitarianism, of course, nothing Marx would recognize;"

"Will the peasants be allowed to keep the land they've been given after you win the battle of the cities? Or is this just a temporary measure to get them on side?"

He didn't care what or even whether she answered: it wasn't her fault if she wasn't interested in abstract questions of political philosophy; it was nothing to be ashamed of, and talking meant he could look her in the face:

"Is it true women are really free now, really the equal of men?"

She nodded vigorously, and he decided to see if she could be teased:

"I mean, I know you can't be bought and sold any more, that dowries are prohibited and all children legitimate, but could you ask a man to marry you? And if it didn't work out: could you divorce your husband?"

"I am not thinking of getting married," she said: "What Lao Kou said the other night: was not right..."

"Ah, yes..." said Ed, inwardly exulting at the possibilities opened up by this piece of priceless information, eager - too eager - to push further:

"Lao Kou told me you need to have tests, perhaps medicines...?"

"What?!" she gasped and Ed realized what a bloody fool he'd been. All right: Lao Kou would now definitely be in the shits for discussing her with him, but for now that was the end of that attempt at conversation, and he scolded himself: haven't you learned anything about these people?

That noon, when - as was now clearly her custom - she spent the time productively, pulling a little notebook out of her breast pocket and sitting apart, talking to herself, doggedly learning the ten characters she'd set herself for the day, he offered to help her, eager to get his hands on that notebook that nestled so close to her heart... He even offered to teach her the new Latin alphabet of 28 letters the Reds were experimenting with, if she was interested. Which she wasn't - and he didn't blame her: dumb idea.

That night they stayed in a peasant hut, the boys on the kang, Ed on the doors outside; the girl as usual squirreled away somewhere. They killed and cooked a chicken for him, wouldn't take any money: "we can't have a foreign devil telling people in the outside world that we Reds have no etiquette" he heard the woman say to the girl as she led her away. Ed wondered what other etiquette she might suggest to her... He watched the children scampering around the compound among the goats and pigs, but when the woman tried to bring one of them over to him to say hello, the child burst into tears. They offered him tobacco and a long bamboo pipe and then lit the rape-seed oil lamps.

He declined to go with them to huddle round the new village radio in the new village school, stayed behind, blew smoke rings: he could settle down in a place like this; she could get a job in the textile mill or the school and he'd work for The Red China Daily News. He'd build them a little thatched cottage down by the river, blue moonflowers over the porch; he'd grow beans and squash and peppers, and she'd hum to herself in the courtyard as she ground apricot shells with hemp when the baby had a cough. Who needs electricity anyway? Who needs movies and hot showers, coffee and ice cream when you've got good health, clean mountain air, freedom, dignity, hope, a soul-mate?

And then they were off to the front, Ed with a borrowed automatic and an escort of ten Red troopers armed with Mausers, the girl riding bare-back, the sun turning her hair to black jade. Eagles and buzzards flew overhead and a herd of graceful gazelles came near, sniffed the air and then swooped off with incredible speed and grace. Ed didn't know why it made him feel so deeply sad. After five hours they reached the ancient Mohammedan city of Yu Wang with its glazed yellow-brick mosque. Yu Wang had only recently been liberated, its walls pockmarked with bullets, its inhabitants scarred by the atrocities of the Kuomintang who had rounded up the entire population of five hundred families, publicly tortured the headman, divided up the young girls and women among themselves, and then machine-gunned the rest on the principle that when you can't tell a Red from a good citizen, you kill them all. Outside the town, they saw a peasant hut up on a hillside with smoke curling from a chimney, climbed up and found the only occupant to be an old man who had gone insane. The girl knelt down and tried to comfort him but all he could do was sit, arms round his knees, rocking back and forth, murmuring "Allah Akhbar, Allah Akhbar."

Many of the troops up here were Mohammedans, with luxuriant dark beards and big swords with which they could demonstrate a dozen different ways to remove your enemy's head. They demonstrated on watermelons and afterwards ate them, spitting out the seeds as they swore oaths against the local warlord: that "motherfucker Ma Hung-kuei: he taxes your shit."

That night - because she found Ed less pushy than the young soldiers and also because she rather mistrusted the Mohammedans, she left with him when he went outside for his customary smoke. Went some distance away, having only one pack of Camels left and not wanting to appear too selfish.

They walked off into the night. Crickets chirped from the thorn-bushes. A flock of wild geese pierced a lonely cloud.

They sat down in the lee of the mosque, and Ed asked her why she didn't like the Mohammedans.

"These people here, these Hue peoples," she answered: "I don't know if we'll be able to trust them if it comes to a conflict between their religion and our politics. You," she turned to him: "You I think are a water-melon: green outside but red inside. These peoples here, I fear, are radishes."

It was the nicest thing she'd ever said to Ed. When she leaned back against the crumbling wall and concluded: "You can't have two loves," he leapt in: "What about Lao Kou then?"

"Lao Kou," she said, frowning: "Lao Kou talks too much. If I marry him it is only because his bad thoughts interfere with his work."

And then, as he watched, she reached up and pulled the elastic bands out of her plaits. The hair fell loose, and she shook her head, ran her fingers through her hair, teasing out the tangles, then pensively twisted the ends into spirals round her slender fingers. She leaned back and Ed was sure he saw her smile then, melting softly into the moonlight.

It was a crescent moon, a waning moon. A single bird flew across it, its beak seeming to penetrate it, tail slowly disengaging as it winged its way towards a star...

He never forgot that moment, filed the whole scene away in his collection of what he called "magic moments:" those charmed moments when a flower opens, when time seems to skip a beat, when you suddenly see something familiar as if for the first time.

The difference was that he always knew those other moments were inherently transient... But I know that about this girl too - really. Don't I? Deep down. Know it's impossible. Already she's replaited her hair, is cracking sunflower seeds with her sharp little white teeth, the shells cringing.

He knew it was hopeless. He wasn't a doctor like George Hatem, and what use is a journalist who can't file his stories? She couldn't come back with him: there was Peg for a start and, in any case, what could she be: his native mistress? Live in the back room with the goldfish and go for a walk at night with the pet dog...? She couldn't live there, he couldn't live here, could never really be part of it. All he could do was envy those who were.

And so when he was informed, back in Yu Wang, that two divisions were preparing to march South and meet up with Chu Teh, and that the girl was to go with them, that he could accompany them only part of the way, he did not put up much of a fight. They gave him a fine Ninghsia pony with sleek flanks and well-filled buttocks, and a captured Western saddle instead of the narrow wooden one, but he chose to walk. It went more slowly that way. A Nanking bomber appeared, but the men just melted quietly into the tall grass, their wide, grass camouflage hats obliterating them, only the horsemen in danger as the frisky ponies shied and bolted. The plane circled twice, dropped an iron egg, and flew away.

All morning, a pack of thirty or so wild Kansu greyhounds - lithe, graceful, delicate - ran alongside them, occasionally dashing off to chase a gazelle or a prairie hog. Quite a lot of the soldiers had animals as pets, took them everywhere with them: a monkey on a leash, a slate-gray pet pigeon perched on a shoulder, little white mice peeking out of pockets. On the roadside, peasants hawked fruit and melons, and one young soldier traded in his pet rabbit for three melons, but after he'd eaten them, he was very dour, wanting his rabbit back.

Ed took his last pictures. He liked to keep the reels of film bundled up together with the relevant notes and now went round his escort, miming: a piece of string...? No...? He left her to last, looked her in the eyes, did his mime, grinning and nodding at her plaits. At first she didn't understand: she wasn't used to men standing that close to her - and making all those faces as well... Ah... She reached behind her neck and pulled the elastic band out of one of her plaits.

He bowed - "Xie xie" - took the elastic band from her and backed away.

Placing the elastic band safely in his breast pocket, he tied up the papers and film with a shoe lace. Then he went around saying his farewells - especially to the little Red Devils, the cheeky, cheerful, plucky children he'd come to love: "I suspected," he wrote, "that more than once an older man, looking at them, forgot his pessimism and was heartened to think that he was fighting for the future of lads like those. Seeing them made you feel that China was not hopeless, that no nation is more hopeless than its youth."

He hoped to have a final moment with her, but one of the Red Devils took him aside. Shang Chi-pang was the 'Beau Brummell' of the Vanguards, always snappily dressed, the peak of his cap regularly refilled with cardboard whenever it broke or just bent. He had a problem: his given name - Chi-pang - sounds very much like 'chi-pa' which, unfortunately, means 'penis.' Solemnly he handed Ed a scrap of paper on which his name was neatly written:

"Comrade Snow," he said: "When you write about me for the foreign papers, I hope you won't make any mistake in my name: it would give a bad impression to foreign comrades if they thought a Red soldier was named 'chi-pa!"

Ed tells that story in Red Star: "Until then I had no intention of introducing him into this book, but with that remark he walked straight into it - right beside the Generalissimo."

The girl's story he doesn't tell, didn't include. Not because he didn't know it: before she rode away, she kept her part of the bargain: she handed him her small notebook - in which she told her story, up to that point.

When they parted, standing, holding the reins of their ponies, the escort at a discreet distance, he wanted to reach out and stroke her raven hair, pull her into his arms, fall at her feet. Trembling, he tried to give her his camera, having some vague idea that perhaps in that way they could remain in touch. But she wouldn't take it, only very reluctantly accepting instead a pen:

"If you ever need someone, if you ever need help..."

"Thank you," she said: "I won't..."

He rode away.

He didn't look back.

It hurt too much.

Green Waters Run Deep

"For a moment there, I was afraid you were really going to fall."

"I'm a rubber ball, Chairman. When I fall, I bounce."

"Not if you fall in water...?" says Mao, watching her change out of her costume.

"No: in water I make a big splash..."

Mao laughs. It isn't a boisterous laugh: he isn't like that. It's an approving laugh: it says this woman can match me, is as smart as she is desirable...

He doesn't have any doubts about who is the fish and who is the fisherman...

"You must go and change," he says, turning away but then fixing her with one teasing eye: "But don't change too much. We must meet again."

"Yes. There are many gaps in my understanding..."

Lan Ping knew how to flatter, how to please, how to charm. That doesn't mean she was insincere: just because she could act emotions doesn't mean she didn't feel them.

When the invitation comes, she dresses carefully - neither too coquettish nor too demure. She's seen his wife: pale, wild-eyed, skinny Zizhen, dry as a bamboo cane. Clearly this man could exhaust his women and did: wear them out. But Lan Ping didn't steal Mao from Zizhen as her enemies would later accuse. There had already been violent rows, chairs thrown across the room. Zizhen had caught him one night with Lily Wu in the cave of that foreign woman, drinking wine and writing couplets, talking about love and about poetry: romantic poetry. They jumped up when the door flew open: the Amazon confronted the Princess, and turned on the Emperor:

"Bastard! Son of a pig. How dare you sneak up here and sleep with that bourgeois bitch!"

She began to hit him with her flashlight; Mao didn't resist, sitting still in greatcoat and cotton cap as the blows rained down. When she stopped, he said calmly:

"You're ruining yourself, Zizhen, disgracing yourself as a Communist. Go home before your comrades learn about this."

But she was out of control, turned on the cowering Lily:

"Dancing whore! How dare you try your filthy tricks on our chairman," and flew at her, scratching her face, pulling her hair.

Mao said: "You're behaving like a rich woman in an American movie," and turned to his bodyguard: "Take her home."

It took three strong men to pin her, restrain her, carry her down the hill, Mao walking silently behind, startled faces watching the procession from the shadows.

As was the proper procedure, Mao reported the incident to the Party the next morning. They interviewed Zizhen, who declared that Lily Wu had alienated the affections of her husband, demanded she be sent away, banished, so should the foreign woman, all foreigners...

Mao didn't object; he didn't want Lily Wu any more: you don't shack up with the woman who destroys your marriage. But he didn't want Zizhen either. There was a vacancy...

"Your wife?" enquires Lan Ping as she steps into the cave.

"Has had to go to Moscow. For treatment."

"Ah."

"You will stay - for dinner?"

Lan Ping nods and, as Mao feeds her sea slugs and bear paws captured from the Kuomintang, she feeds him her aphrodisiac of flattering questions.

After the guard clears the table and leaves, Mao offers to show her his poems.

When he stands up to get them, she notices that he has a tear in his trousers and offers to repair them for him...

Afterwards they lie on the kang and smoke.

So when Ed got back from the front, he found that Mao had moved. Something else had changed too - or perhaps now he just noticed it more: what they called, tongue in cheek, the "undisciplined guerrilla activity" every night as young soldiers and newly arrived girls slipped down to the bushes by the river. There had already been one nasty incident: Huang Kegong, a veteran of the Long March, had fallen in love with a sixteen-year old student; when she refused to marry him, he shot her dead, claiming she had "mocked the sincere love of a revolutionary soldier." The tribunal punished him but also criticized the girl for "flirting without the intention of marrying."

Ed decided it was time to get out: if he stayed much longer he might see things, learn things he didn't want to know - and which they might not want him to report.

Mao's new cave had a fresh vegetable patch outside, planted with garlic, beans, squash, red peppers. The cave itself was larger, deeper, with whitewashed walls, bookcases and an incongruous Victrola gramophone. Mao was sitting eating peanuts and sunflower seeds, cracking the shells open with his teeth and spitting the husks on the floor to mingle promiscuously with the cigarette butts.

A woman came in: she had short hair and dark, flashing eyes and Ed was sure he'd met her somewhere before.

Mao says laconically:

"This is Jiang Qing."

The woman comes over and shakes Ed's hand.

So this is the woman everyone's talking about? The temptress, the new Empress... It is said that when the Party, out of respect and admiration for what Zizhen had been, took her side, Mao went to them himself and issued his own ultimatum:

"Without the love of Lan Ping, I cannot go on with the revolution. If you resist my wishes, I will go back to my native village with Lan Ping and become a farmer."

After all, marriage is now supposed to be by consent, is it not, and divorce by request...?

The woman - now renamed "Green Waters" - is holding out a plate with fresh-cooked red peppers:

"Zedong grows them himself," she says smiling across at Mao like a newly-wed.

"Sit down," says Mao to Ed, but when he turns, he sees that the woman has already taken the chair he used to occupy.

He gets a stool from the wall and moves it over to the table.

Mao says:

"I suppose you've heard what they're saying about me?"

"I..."

"Of course you have: it's your job. And you're supposed to be good at it."

"I don't write up rumors, if that's what you're..."

"As you can see: they are not all rumors."

Mao has a quizzical look on his face, which Ed can't read. He realizes how much power over him this man has. Enough for him never to get out, to disappear...

But Mao smiles his benevolent Buddha-smile:

"You must write whatever you think you must write. Of course, there would be many different ways of telling it. This...'new arrangement' for example: it could be written up as an aging man's self-indulgence, or a new phase in the struggle - for which I need a different kind of partner."

"And you'd prefer the latter version?"

"Mr. Snow: I do not ask your advice about my military tactics, so I will not give you advice about how to be a good American journalist. The first version would give comfort to the enemy: it would give them ammunition to use against us..."

"Yes, I understand. You know, Chairman: you didn't need to say any of that: I told you when I came: I am a friend..."

Mao grunts, spits another peanut shell on the floor; Jiang Qing tut-tuts at him and Mao smiles at her apologetically. Ed looks at the two of them, engrossed in each other's eyes in the soft candlelight. The Man seems to have found what he was looking for...

"Now don't look so glum," says Jiang Qing to Ed: "We are going dancing tonight. You will come, of course. Zedong has learned to dance."

She turns to the Man, who takes her hand and lets her pull him up out of his chair.

Ed says he needs to pack his things, has an early start in the morning. They shake hands and Mao says:

"And you, friend? Did you get everything you wanted?"

"Well, no," says Ed, "but I think I'd have to stay here for the rest of my life to do that..."

"Then it's time you went back..."

PART THREE

RED SUNSET

"Between the idea
And the reality,
Between the conception
And the creation
Falls the shadow."

T.S. Eliot,
The Hollow Men

On October 31st, I was called to a meeting with the leadership.

Three people were waiting for me: Luo, the chief administrator of the Institute - a tall, pale, nervous, rather sickly man who had signed my contract; Wang, the head of the Workers Propaganda Team - stocky, blunt, bristle-chinned - and Yen Wei, my liaison comrade - who looks away when I walk in.

We sit in soft, deep armchairs with brown dust-covers, smoke cigarettes, drink tea, exchange polite conversation: do I need more cotton coupons, am I drinking lots of hot water? Then Luo coughs, picks up an envelope, hands it to me:

"Here are your tickets."

"What?"

"Your railway tickets. Travel permits. Hotel vouchers."

"Oh wow: thank you..."

Too soon: the tickets and the hotel voucher are for the seaside: Bei Dai He...

I look up:

"But... Yenan?"

"Da Wei and his family will be more comfortable in Bei Dai He."

"Didn't you get my memo? About going to Yenan?"

"We have just given him our reply to that memo."

"But..."

"There are no trains to Yenan."

"Oh, come on... I happen to know that..."

Luo's hands tremble and his voice shakes:

"I am a member of the Communist Party of China. Members of the Communist Party of China do not tell lies..."

I stare at him: the word he's used - "huang" - if spoken with a different tone, means nervous, timid, fearful; also curtain or screen; even yellow.

"I never said you lied."

"We are pleased that Da Wei agrees to go to Bei Dai He."

"But I don't..."

"He does not like the seaside?"

"I can't swim..."

"There is an instructor there, he will help you..."

"It's not the point. I'd rather not go on vacation at all..."

"He must go on his vacation: it is in his contract..."

"I signed that contract because I believed..."

"We cannot know what he believes and what he does not believe. He signed the contract and must now go on vacation to Bei Dai He."

They say "he" all the time: it is subtle this - the use of the third person: we could be discussing someone else. Once we can get him out of the way, all will be well...

I have to keep reminding myself that the other person is me:

"I came to China to study your revolution. Where better to do that than in Yenan, Hunan, Chingkanshan... The route of the Long March..."

"He can see all that in the Museum of the Revolution."

"I didn't think the revolution belonged in a museum. Yet..."

"It is very hot in Chingkanshan at this time of year..."

"We lived in Malaysia. Surely it's not hotter than..."

"Malaysia is not a socialist country."

And so it goes on: for four hours. They are rigid, unbending. They do not even fidget.

I get up:

"Even in Russia I had more freedom of movement than here..."

It's just as well the fan wasn't on because the shit just hit it:

"He must not say that Russia is a more free country than China; he must not insult the Chinese people, the Party..."

And the meeting breaks up.

I collect Tracey from the kindergarten:

"Did you do anything special today?"

"Oh yes, we learned a new song. About the Mouse Who Sings..."

"The what?"

"Mao Tzu-xi..."

Chairman Mao?

"I can't wait to go to the cave where he lived... Will there be dinosaurs too?"

Tracey has begun to dream about Chairman Mao and has put a picture of him on the wall of her bedroom. There had been long and acrimonious debates about that picture during the Cultural Revolution: about whether the mole on his chin should be painted out, made smaller, have a long white hair growing out of it, which among traditional Chinese is a sign of wisdom...

"Why does Chairman Mao have a spotty face?"

"It's not a spot..."

"He should eat his vegetables."

"It's a mole."

"What's a mole?"

"A sort of blemish..."

"Will I have a mole when I grow up?"

"Maybe. Some people have them, others don't. Some say they cause cancer..."

"Chinese people?"

"All people."

"Why is China called China?"

"Because they once had an Emperor called Chin."

"Chin? Did he have a mole too?"

"No, I don't think so. Moles don't only grow on chins. Everyone is different. Chin was his name."

"That's not a name."

"Yes, it is, I expect it means something."

"What does Chairman Mao mean?"

"Well Mao means hair..."

"Hair?"

"And Chairman means he's the leader."

"Leader...?"

She marches round the room, arms stiff, chanting "Yi-er, yi-er, one-two, one-two" and then stops:

"Where's he leading us?"

I wish I could answer that: before we came here I could have answered it, but now:

"What do you think about the editorial in The People's Daily today?" I ask my class.

They look at me, at each other; Dong Ming says:

"It tells us that…"

"Yes, Dong Ming, I know what it says, I read it. What do you think about it?"

"At the moment we are busy studying this question under the guidance of Chairman Mao's directives…"

"Yes, it says that here too. But what do you think about it? Don't you have any feelings about it?"

"I feel we should think about it carefully."

I fidget in my chair, a fly buzzes against the impenetrable flywire in the window:

"Look, I'll tell you what I think about it and then…"

He waits patiently until I've finished, then he says:

"Chairman Mao teaches us that a person's standpoint is a reflection of his class background. We are a socialist country and so we see things from a Marxist-Leninist viewpoint. You, I see, have difficulty doing this so I will try to help you. What the article says is…"

And, after he's picked up the paper and read the article back to me, word for word, he looks up triumphantly:

"Now, does that answer your problem?"

Because it's me who has the problem. If I don't understand something or agree with it, it is up to me to find a way to accept it.

"Is it wrong to criticize?"

"No, it is right to criticize what is not correct. But sometimes it is hard to say what is correct and what isn't. So it is best not to criticize: it may not be correct…"

It strikes me that if people wanted to oppose Mao, to sabotage the Cultural Revolution, they would not attack him or his ideas directly - unless they were bored with life. They would make him boring, bring China to a state of verbal suffocation, intellectual constipation and self-lobotomy.

It's called performing a "snow job" on yourself.

Yen Wei alone seems different:

"You must not take it personally," she says: "It is not about you. We too cannot go where we like, live where we like. We have to have a permit, a "hukou" which specifies where we can live. Without it we can't buy food, register a child in school. So many people wandered around and caused so much trouble in the Cultural Revolution..."

"And it's not going to happen again. Is it? It's over, and there isn't going to be a new one?"

She doesn't answer.

"What happened, Yen Wei: why is everyone so... cagey, so cautious, afraid to take a stand? Why all the screens, the curtains? It's not supposed to be like that. Is it?"

She is looking at the books in my bookshelf: Fanshen, The Long March, Red Star Over China...

She says: "May I?"

"Of course."

It's the Pelican edition of Ed's book, the one with Mao's picture on the front, sporting a military cap with a red star. Ed's cap actually: he lent it to Mao when he took that picture.

She flicks the pages: she has never seen it before. Red Star was secretly published in China in 1937 under the title "Foreign Journalist's Impressions of the Northwest." Five thousand copies circulated clandestinely but since 1949 it has been impossible to get a copy even of that version anywhere in China.

She is looking through the Index in the back, where Snow placed the Biographical Notes of all the people mentioned in the text.

I've already looked: there's nothing under Yen Wei. But then he did leave a lot out: like any historian, any journalist, he selected which facts to report, selected them according to what he wanted to say - just like a novelist does with a plot.

His archives contain reams and reams of notes, jottings, sketches, drafts of things he never put in the book...

"Did you meet Edgar Snow, when you were in Yenan?"

She closes the book.

"Listen, Yen Wei: since I can't go there myself; you'll have to tell me what it's like. Or rather what it was like - back then... Would you like to borrow the book?"

She shakes her head, puts it back, but I've made copies of parts of it for my class - and of a story I found.

It had no title.

I called it "How The Swallow Lost Its Tail."

I

"I got it! Look!"

He spills the contents of his bag on the floor: a dozen thick diaries, bulging notebooks, thirty reels of film...

"This is going to cause a sensation, Peg."

His face is gaunt under a red, bristling beard; he begins to dance around the room:

"This changes everything..."

"So what's he like?"

Peg bends down to help him - gingerly, with the tips of her fingers only, extricating and then tossing all his filthy clothes to one side. They are stained yellow-brown and stink of horses, stale sweat, wood smoke, other smells she can't exactly identify.

Ed is kneeling on the floor, on the carpet, a battered Red Army cap pushed back from his forehead, stroking his precious notebooks:

"I nearly lost them..."

"What?"

"When I jumped down from the truck smuggling us back over the lines, my bag was missing. All my interviews, diaries and notebooks, the first photographs ever taken of Soviet China, the first moving pictures of the Red Army: all gone."

The truck had been transporting gunny sacks, full of broken rifles being sent in for repair; to conceal Ed's bag from suspicious Kuomintang sentries and nosy gendarmes, it had been stuffed in one of those sacks. Twenty miles back, they'd all been thrown off the truck at the arms depot...

They had to go back - Ed distraught, frantic, fearing sabotage, but they retrieved the bag - intact, its contents scattered now over the floor of his house in Peking:

"What's he like?" says Ed, sitting up: "A dreamer, a warrior, ideologist, revolutionary, poet..."

He laughs:

"He's grotesque really. I mean, there he sits, two pairs of cotton pants to his name, and yet he speaks as if he holds some irrevocable mandate to save China. As if he alone knows what her future is and how to make it happen. But then, you see, Peg: he does: he's worked out exactly what's going to happen, how he's going to win. I tell you, if self-belief is all you need..." he laughs: "He's got - what did Mark Twain call it? The confidence of a Christian with four aces..."

He looks up: he could still be back in the cave, Mao spitting out seed husks, grinding ink:

"You know what he calls the Chinese people? Blank pieces of paper. You know where he says he gets his generals from? He says he makes them out of mud... He's either going to get a lot of egg on his face or become a very very great man. And this," he says, patting the notebooks possessively: "this is going to make him famous."

"Not only him," says Peg, getting to her feet, kicking his filthy clothes into some sort of order, then calling for a servant to take them out and wash them.

Peg is jealous. Relieved too: the AP had put out a story that Ed had been kidnapped by Red bandits who had caught him snooping on them and executed him. His father had cabled, having read the story of his death in the Kansas City Star.

"The reports of my death are premature," says Ed as he wolfs down half a dozen scrambled eggs and a huge jug of coffee with milk.

"Good to be home?" says Peg.

Ed pushes Gobi the dog away from nuzzling his crotch. Home? Has he come home, or left it behind?

He gets up, goes out into the courtyard for a smoke. The caged birds are singing evensong and he feels strangely depressed, flat. Why is achievement so empty compared to striving; why is possessing so much less than wanting, dreaming so much more vivid than waking up? I should be elated: this is the story I've been chasing for seven years: why this sense of loss?

He grunts: the best stories are always written in the past tense, aren't they?

Red Star Over China was completed in July 1937, just as the first Japanese troops entered Peking, heralding eight years of vicious, brutal, inhuman war. The book made Mao famous, it's success surpassing even Ed's wettest dreams: it was "an epic story, superbly told," wrote The Times; "intensely readable, an extraordinary book, every page significant," chimed in The Herald: "one of the best books of historical journalism ever written." "No Westerner since Marco Polo has so profoundly influenced our attitudes towards China as Ed Snow." His picture beamed from the cover of the Saturday Review of Literature: everything was going his way, even the Japanese his allies, their attack perfect timing because it made "headlines on the front pages of every American newspaper - which act as an advertisement for our book," his American publisher Bennett Cerf cabled him, and promptly ordered a print run of 100,000 copies. They sold out in the first few weeks, only failing to make Book-of-the-Month because of the veto of a prominent leftist, Heywood Broun. Everyone else took the book to bed with them: Roosevelt, Gandhi, Hemingway, even Shirley Temple had a copy. A coffee company jumped on the bandwagon, running an ad featuring a picture Ed had taken of Mao and Chu Teh seated at a table on which one of their coffee cans was prominently displayed. Ed didn't tell them it was being used as an ash-tray.

But though everyone loved it, no-one got pregnant by it. Readers are as selective as writers, and though everyone read it, all anyone found in it was what they wanted to find, what they were looking for. Ed had hoped that Red Star would rouse the world and especially America to rally behind Mao, help him defeat the Japanese. But what America read was that Mao could keep the Japanese so bogged down that they would never be able to invade the colonies the West had scattered like seed all over Asia. The West could relax: Mao would save their Empires for them! Admiral Harry Yarnell, commander of the US Pacific fleet, told Ed that Mao "sounds like a good old-fashioned patriot to me." Marine Captain Evans Carlson, who later became so famous in the Pacific War, declared that the Red Army was "a unique example of Christian ethics and brotherhood in practice."

The only negative reviews appeared in the left-wing press, Ed's caustic critiques of the USSR exposing him as a "Trotskyist." It was a charge Ed resented and, more so, felt endangered the success of his book, "Trotskyist" being synonymous in Left-wing circles with "traitor." He despised the American left as arse-lickers to the Kremlin, forever polishing the sun. But they were influential - especially among the book-reading American public: Ed cut out whole paragraphs and agreed to make "corrections" to his more "inflammatory" comments. Moscow had a similar, though more drastic solution: they published a heavily censored version of Red Star under the title "Heroic People of China:" it came complete with an introduction with quotations from "the great Stalin" setting out the "correct line for its readers."

They weren't the only people to revise his story: Ed himself began to lose faith. When Chiang was kidnapped in Sian and released only after he'd signed up for a United Front, Ed concluded that Mao had "buckled under to the Kuomintang," had "thrown in the sponge:" "we can expect little more from the Red leadership." But what really bugged him was that this new alliance muddied the distinction he wanted to make between the corrupt Chiang and the clean Mao: "it weakens the whole structure of my book!"

And it didn't help when Chou En-lai personally requested Ed to delete all the anti-Chiang remarks and anecdotes in Red Star:

"Hell, it's all material Chou himself gave me last year! It weakens my whole argument!"

But, again, he submitted. He went even further than that: Ed buttered up to Chiang Kai-shek too, publishing articles in which he called him "courageous, decisive, determined and responsible;" "a great leader." But by then Ed had his own solution for China's ills and needed Chiang's support. Because, deep down, Ed never shared Mao's vision, and though he warmed himself in the reflected fame,

Ed was neither the first nor the last to think he could make love to himself in the light of a distant star and not go blind.

He had always feared what could happen if Mao ever did gain outright control of China, foreseeing - prophetically - that "the new regime will have to enlist the present bureaucrats to be able to govern at all, and ensure their loyalty by granting them special status and rewards so that a new privileged class will replace the exploiting class and will not voluntarily, any more than any ruling class in history, carry out measures for its own destruction or liquidation."

Mao himself had told Ed what he thought of bureaucrats: "They are conceited, complacent, subjective and one-sided, they do not listen to people. They must be thrown in the shit-bucket." But Ed understood that a planned economy needs bureaucrats like a latrine needs bacteria. The phenomenal success of Red Star convinced him that he could influence events, shape history, but it also made him feel guilty: "I made the shattering discovery that what a man writes or says, can lead people, even complete strangers, to actions which might end in speedy death. I felt personally answerable to the Chinese whose lives I had wittingly or unwittingly helped to place in peril. As I heard of friends and students killed in the war I realized that my own writing had taken on the nature of political action."

It was time to come out, assume responsibility, come up with an alternative: he called it The Chinese Industrial Co-Operative Scheme. Indusco for short.

It was to be socialism without Marx: if it succeeded, it would make revolution unnecessary.

"The idea itself is simple," he told Sir Archibald Clark-Kerr, the British Ambassador, courting his support: "Japan controls virtually all of China's industrial capacity, her chemical, rubber and cement factories, the mines, the railways. But thousands of Chinese workers have fled the cities, are displaced, wandering aimlessly. Indusco will employ them, behind the lines, create thousands of small factories organized as co-operatives in which everyone has a share, a stake."

"It's not Communism, of course," said Sir Archibald Clark-Kerr laconically: "If so, England would already be a Commie paradise. Scandinavia too."

He leaned back and lit his pipe:

"So, Mr. Snow: you want to make a co-operative commonwealth out of China and cheat the class war. Is that it?"

"It does not seem desirable for the Communist Party to replace the Kuomintang," said Ed: "If they did, the West might take active steps to close China entirely as a capital market."

But cheating Mao of his revolution and cheating Chiang were two very different things: even as Indusco expanded, setting up clinics, printing houses, opening up small mines, the Chiang family diverted the funds to their private accounts, using it to launder money, creaming off their cut. In the end, it became too much and Ed wrote a cable to the Herald Tribune exposing the Chiang family's corruption. But he showed it first to his friend Nick, who said:

"The facts are true enough, but it may ruin China's chance of getting further American loans if you cable this."

Ed dropped the cable in the wastepaper basket.

But it told: in Pao-An and then Yenan, Ed had glimpsed a vision of a future China, compared to which the present realities now disgusted him even more: "dirt, lice, fleas, flies, bugs, poverty, famine, filth: there is nothing, absolutely nothing worth preserving in this civilization."

As for the Red option: "Red leaders such as Chou En-lai have acquired all the mannerisms of bureaucrats while stationed in the Nationalist capitals," ruling with all "the paternalistic infallibility of a parent." The only reason they didn't quarrel and fight each other was because they were "too busy avoiding extermination by their enemies to work out on each other."

So far...

By late 1941, Ed was drained, sick, emaciated, broke, guilt-ridden, lonely and facing divorce. It was time to leave:

"I would still be for the cause of China... But I would never again imagine that I personally was anything more to her than an alien corn adrift on vast tides of history with a logic of its own and beyond my power to alter or my birthright to judge. I am an American, and now at last I see myself as I am, an Ishmael in a foreign land."

The day before he sailed, he sat out in the courtyard of the now empty house in the lengthening shadows, took something out of his pocket, turned it over and over in his fingers: an elastic band, in it a few hairs...

It was autumn and the swallows were leaving their nests under the curved eaves. Curtly, Ed told the gardener to plug the holes.

Then he looked down at the cat's cradle he'd made of the elastic band:

"And what about you, eh? What happens to you now, I wonder...?"

He had to exorcise her, before he left, exorcise those eyes once and for all, purge her from his still twitching imagination. He knew only one way to do that, one way he was good at: write.

He already has the draft she gave him; all he needs to do is translate it, give it a title.

And add an ending...

Ꮒow Ꭲꭼ Ꮥwallow Ꮮost Ꮖtꜱ Ꭲail: Ꮲart Ꮻne

I was born to a family of poor peasants in January 1919, at the end of the Year of the Horse, one of six children who survived birth. My horoscope was not auspicious: horses kick and, though they make good soldiers, girls born in the Year of the Horse will not find husbands or, if they do, will be widowed young. I think I would have been sold to the landlord to pay off debts or save a brother from the army if one of my uncles had not been sterile. You once said to me how interesting you found it that General Chu Teh had been given away when he was a child; I don't think you understand: how else can a sterile man have someone tend the altar when he dies? Without one, he'll spend eternity as a hungry ghost, forever wandering, aimlessly...

My parents had already given Uncle my younger brother: I was sent along to care for him, stop him crying, change his pants and be useful to Auntie around the house. When Uncle became senile, they would find me a husband to make me pregnant so that I could feed Uncle fresh breast milk.

I was thirteen when the Blue Shirts came to the village and rounded up everyone with the name Hsu. I thanked heaven that our name had been changed, but my brother grabbed a brush and ink and a piece of board and was next seen walking down the main street with the board tied round his neck, calling out aloud what he'd written on it in case the soldiers couldn't read:

"I too am Hsu."

No-one dared run and stop him, not even my Uncle. We just stood and watched as he walked along the dusty street towards the man with the skull-face and drawn sword. Even the dogs held their breath. My Uncle pulled my head into his gown but my left eye still saw how the little, sturdy body took three or four more steps even after its head lay in the dust, staring wide-eyed...

After that, my Auntie treated me as a slave. She was a heavy smoker of opium, but I hated the smell of it and one night, when I could stand it no more, I got up and kicked a pan of her opium from the stove. She was furious, called a meeting of the whole clan and demanded my death by drowning as an unfilial child. But my Uncle stepped in and said: "Why waste her? She has cost us good money" - so they sold me instead. I didn't mind: anything would be better than staying in that miserable village with the ghost of my brother - even joining a theatre company, but instead I was sold to a family of professional mourners. Such families were doing good business in Shanghai and needed new recruits. But although they beat me and starved me, they could not make me wail. I would do everything else: wear sackcloth, burn paper money, bang the cymbals or walk on stilts, but I would not wail and I would not cry.

One day a funeral was disrupted when some students stopped the procession in the street. It was the funeral of a girl who had been married to an old man chosen for her by her parents: sitting in the bridal sedan chair, she had pulled out a razor and slit her own throat. The students stopped the funeral procession and turned it into a demonstration against family oppression and the evils of the old society.

When someone yelled "The gendarmes are coming" and they turned and left, I followed them. They tried to wave me back but I just stopped and, when they moved on, followed at a distance.

They let me stay with them - on a straw mattress in the back room of a small bookshop, sending me out to distribute leaflets in the streets. I couldn't read, which is one reason they chose me: if I was caught, I could say truthfully that I didn't know what was written on them. It made no difference: one day three men stopped me in the street, grabbed my leaflets, read them, yelled at me, dragged me away, dunked my head in pepper water until it came out of my ears and when I still wouldn't tell them who gave me the leaflets, took me to a back room, tied my hands and arms tight behind my back and then hoisted me up to hang from the rafters like an aeroplane.

After every day of torture, I decided that the next time they came for me, I would confess, but when they came and strung me up, I decided I would wait until they let me down...

I do not want to say what they did to me next, but afterwards they threw me out in the street, dripping with water, sweat, blood and other fluids, my head shaved raw.

After a few months, my belly began to swell. I didn't want the child: it was the child of a devil, a devil who had hurt me badly. The students took me to a Western doctor, but he said I was a healthy girl, so they took to me an old woman who gave me a cup of foul-smelling herbs to drink. After it was over, she told me that she'd buried it in a shallow grave where it would be dug up and eaten by a dog or some other animal, for such spirits, she said, are not proper children but evil spirits seeking to insinuate themselves into a household. She gave me a small china vial, the sort you put perfume in, but this one, she said, had the child's putrid bile in it, along with other poisonous juices from a scorpion, a lizard, a centipede, a snake and a toad. I put it away and as I recovered, one of the girl students began to teach me how to read - and more: what the words mean. The first word she taught me was the word for work, or worker: it has only three strokes and looks, as you know, like a letter H lying on its side. The top stroke, she explained, is the sky, the lower one the earth; the vertical stroke joining them is the working class: they stand on the earth but reach up to the sky.

But the sky was not looking down kindly on China: in 1934, my friend was sent with a dozen others to Saratsi to help the famine victims dying from drought. She never came back. When I asked what had happened, they said:

"She's decided that it's no use saving just one or two people; we have to save them all. She's crossed over - to the other side."

I thought at first they meant she'd died but they said no, the opposite: she's joined the Red Army.

When Shanghai fell to the Japanese, I was sent to deliver messages to the guerrillas in the hills of Hunan. One day I met my Auntie in the street: she knew who my new friends were, begged my forgiveness for the past. She said Uncle had died: they couldn't afford a doctor. That was life in those days: you didn't even know what you died from. She was very humble and respectful and I was surprised, but then realized she was just taking out insurance in case we won.

Not that we looked like winning: when the Red Army was encircled and fled West, I went with them. Many times in the next year I thought I would die, the only question was how: possibly a bullet but more likely freeze to death, starve to death, be eaten by bears or wolves, shiver to death from malaria or drain away from dysentery. I nearly drowned in the Tatu River but a comrade pulled me out. I didn't change my clothes for two years, sleeping with them on, the lice keeping me awake so I wouldn't be surprised in my sleep.

At first, they gave me jobs like carrying a sewing machine on my back or scavenging for food, but one day I helped capture a great warehouse of salt and we filled our pockets with it, eating it like sugar. When the owner tried to stop us, I shot him in the knee, and took the dagger he wore in his belt. I used it to keep my hair short. When the boy who had saved me from drowning began to court me: he seemed to think I owed him something. One day he boiled his boots and offered to share the broth with me. Another day he brought me a tiny roasted rat. When we came upon the corpse of a dead horse, it was already stripped clean but I used my dagger to scrape the bones and got a cupful of meat, which I shared with him. Crossing the Grasslands, we found some wild turnips, but he insisted on eating them first to see if they were poisonous or not. When he began to vomit, I threw him on the ground, straddled him and pumped his stomach out. Later he told people he'd proposed to me then and I'd accepted, but all that happened was that he said: "If you sit across me like that, you'll have to marry me."

When the armies of Chairman Mao and Chu Teh were separated, I was used as a courier between them but in December 1936, we too got to Pao-An.

There I met up again with the boy who had saved me from the Tatu River. His name was Lao Kou: he was seventeen, had joined the Reds when he was fourteen. They taught him how to read and write, operate a radio and shoot straight. He asked me to marry him. I told him my horoscope and what had been done to me in Shanghai, thinking that would deter him, but after a couple of days, he came back, said that was old thinking, and asked me again.

There was a Westerner in Pao-An. His name was Hatem: he was a doctor, married to a Chinese woman, an actress, Zhou Sufei. He specialized in venereal disease. He examined me, said I could still have children:

"I know what you're thinking," I remember him saying to me: "You're thinking that you're to blame for what happened to you, that the fault must be yours. Girls like you come here all the time:

they've been raped, but they stand and slap their own faces, say they're at fault for being weak. You're a healthy young woman and you've just got to stop thinking that way."

I never forgot him telling me that; he was certainly more help than the other foreigner, a journalist, who kept pestering me to tell him my story, even got Chairman Mao himself to order me to do so. He and Chairman Mao seemed to have become friends, wearing each other's hat. From the way he looked at me, I was afraid he might ask for me and they would give me to him, so I went to Lao Kou and told him I accepted his proposal.

It was in Yenan and, as we waited in the Party office to register our marriage, I remember Lao Kou flicking on the electric light switch again and again so as to watch the bulb glow at the command of his fingers.

When we got back to Pao-An, Lao Kou wanted to go down to the bushes by the river. There were no quarters for married couples, but I said I was too tired and he was too shy to push me. We were standing in the square when suddenly a light went on: someone had turned on one of the big searchlights which hunted for planes, but now it was shining on the two of us. I grabbed my dagger but then I heard people laughing: General Chu had arranged a party for us - with wine and food and even a gramophone. Chairman Mao came too with his new wife: they looked very happy together and everyone danced until we were so tired we could hardly stand. But no-one wanted the music ever to stop. Then Chu Teh came over to me, a big smile on his face:

"I am not sleeping in my cave tonight, little one. You and Lao Kou: it's for you."

Inside we sat together on the kang, listening to the music still playing outside, watching the single tallow candle burn down. I felt him pull the bands out of my hair, which fell loose...

Afterwards I hid my face from him but he gently took my hands away. He saw I was crying, said he was sorry, but I said:

"No. These are not sad tears."

They had been locked away so long.

I would never need salt in my food ever again.

"What do you think?" I ask the class.

They look down at their desks. Only Dong Ming speaks up:

"This story?" he asks: "Are you going to put it in the new textbook?"

"I don't know yet: what do you think?"

"It is not published in China, I think?"

"No."

"Then why have you given it to us to read?"

"Because it's about China. If there's something wrong in there, something untrue, say so. Or do you think it should be censored?"

"There is no censorship in China."

"There are not many books in the shops..."

"We do not want to read bad books so the shops do not sell them."

Only Yin Wei offers any comment. The Institute has been given two tickets to go and see a Revolutionary Peking Opera. It's called "The White-Haired Girl," but it's not the version I know.

Out in the street, Yin Wei explains:

"The heroine's motive in joining the revolution - that she had been raped by a landlord - was too negative. Revolutionaries don't let themselves be raped."

She pauses and then says: "I think you should consider taking that out of the first part of the story you gave us to translate."

"And what about the second part?" I ask.

She shrugs:

"The author makes it seem as if she felt betrayed," she says: "And of course it is true: people do let you down. But that is their problem. I don't think you should stop believing in people just because some of them let themselves down. If people betray themselves, they are the losers, not you. Is it not so? And now I think you should get back home, you are sick, I think."

We are all sick. It's called "Peking throat" - a parched gorge, aching sinuses and blocked ears caused by the withering dryness of the climate, which splits wood and gives you an electric shock when you try to kiss.

It doesn't help that the radiators in the apartment keep breaking down. They send a plumber who bangs them with a hammer and sighs: "The metal is rotten; it was made during the Great Leap Forward." At night, stumbling into the kitchen to get a drink of water, a hundred little red cockroaches freeze in the sudden glare of the bare bulb and then rush away to hide. I don't know where they go: the attendants shake their heads and say it can't be helped: "The Russians brought them." They are also the reason for the other 'bugs' masquerading as smoke detectors in the ceiling: I have no idea who listens to us, but it makes us cautious in bed.

It's all very petty, of course, but it is of such small, everyday, mundane things that real life is made. You can read the theory anywhere.

Or perhaps not: it is a remarkable fact that the classics - Marx, Lenin, Stalin - contain only the vaguest hints about what life might be like after the revolution. Trotsky had something to say about it, and Engels, but this uncertainty about the future of Utopia preoccupies the weekly political study meetings we have organized for ourselves in the Friendship Guesthouse:

"When everyone shares the same basic values, there will be no need for any formal political apparatus: the state will just wither away…"

"Everyone will share proletarian consciousness…"

"Including the peasants?"

"They must learn proletarian consciousness too: that's what communes are for."

"Bureaucrats?"

"Ah: they need regular cultural revolutions to remould their thinking…"

"And if they don't?"

"Then they can bring the whole thing down, undermine it from within…"

And it's all just a mirage, a gleam in your eye, a black hole to mark the place where a star once imploded…

I go wearily home and put on a record: Bob Dylan is with Louise but having visions of Johanna: "which makes it all seem so sad..."

I don't want to fall out of love. Please... Because I have been here before too. I remember very clearly, one evening in St. Petersburg, getting maudlin drunk on cheap vodka and listening as my host - who turned to theatre when the music died - talks about the "true believers," the tragedy of those who gave up everything to go and live and work in some small provincial backwater for thirty years only to be told that "We have changed our mind." His apartment is in one of those sterile suburbs that ring the city, forty or fifty identical concrete skyscrapers like a graveyard of fossilized phalluses. He has glassed in his tiny balcony and filled it with exotic plants: they remind him of his life in a small provincial town in the Caucasus:

"I did what I could: we all did. We never asked what was in it for us; we did it because it gave our lives meaning, purpose, value..."

He begins to cry silently and it's not just the vodka talking:

"How many of us were there? I don't know: tens, hundreds of thousands. We were ready for any sacrifice. Except one: to be told at the end that it had all been a mistake, that there is only one system which works and it is time now to catch up with the West."

He changes the record, puts on "Turandot:" the slave girl is pleading with the prince not to try to solve the Chinese princess's riddles, for it will cost him his life...

But this can't happen in China, can it? They kicked the Russians out, didn't they, rewrote the theory...?

Though I fear I already know the answer, and that it will hurt, it is time to find out.

On November 5th, I was summoned to another meeting with the leadership.

There are two students representing the masses, Old Luo representing the leadership, and Wang the Party. Yin Wei is not there.

I'm not sure who I'm meant to be representing. But I've brought my Little Red Book with me just in case.

Old Luo, as usual, opens the discussion:

"We have studied Da Wei's memorandum on the teaching of phonetics and have decided that, though much that he says is true, we will still teach it - in accordance with Chairman Mao's instruction that every question has two sides."

I nod: I had written the memo because the students here begin their study of English with ten weeks of "Fee, Fi, Fo, Fum; Ma, Mo, Me, My, Moo..." It's not a very scientific way to teach language and I have suggested replacing it with live conversation - and because, as I now repeat to Old Luo:

"Vowels in English are not neutral, they're class based. You can tell where someone in England comes from - and what class they come from - by their vowels. I mean, anyone listening to me knows instantly that I'm a working-class Cockney..."

"Da Wei does not speak proper English? This is a problem..."

"There is no proper English, that's what I'm telling you: as one class becomes dominant their pronunciation becomes the norm. The only person I know who ever denied this was Stalin - no, seriously: read his 1950 essay in which he argues that language is classless. He's wrong: phonetics perpetuates a bourgeois pronunciation. The whole method you've been practicing here is pure Stalin."

It was the first time I'd seen Old Luo gasp. If what I'm saying is right, then it's Cultural Revolution time again at the Peking Institute of Broadcasting! Dunce caps and self-criticism. Or is what I'm saying just another gratuitous insult from this round-eye who dared say he had more freedom in Russia than in China? What was he doing in Russia, in any case?

"Shall I go over my points now, one by one?" I ask.

"It is not necessary: they have already been discussed."

"May I tell the students...?"

"It is not necessary: they have already been told."

"But I have not heard their replies."

"The students have discussed the question and reported their views to us. Now we are telling you. This is called combining democracy with centralism."

"I see. All right, but let us not pretend that we are here to discuss anything then…"

"The decision has been taken, but we can still have a discussion. So that everyone understands…"

"I thought that, in a democratic system, discussion preceded decision-making?"

"We have different views on democracy. In the West, I know you end with a vote."

He looks round at the others:

"Shall we have a vote now?"

Everyone laughs.

Even me.

The students leave, but Luo gestures for me to stay.

He hands me an envelope; I open it: tickets to Bei Dai He.

He says:

"Does Tracey like ice-cream?"

"Yes…?"

"The best ice cream in China is made in Bei Dai He…"

"But it's the middle of winter…?!"

"Yes: is she wearing enough clothes: five layers…?"

"She has a bad throat."

"You should take her to the doctor: your contract includes free medical care."

"Well, yes, but it doesn't actually work that way, does it. We still have to pay a fee whenever we go to the doctor's."

"That is an administrative fee. Anyway, you earn more than the Chinese: you can afford it."

"Then pay me the same salary as the Chinese teachers and treat me like them."

"That is not possible: you need more money - your expenses are higher…"

"Why can't you just treat us all the same?"

"Equal pay for equal work is a bourgeois fallacy."

I smile - or rather my lips do, my heart is not smiling: "Old Luo, I do not want to argue about any of this. But really we have no wish to go to the seaside in the middle of winter…"

"If he does not go, he will be breaking his contract."

"Old Luo, please understand: I am not concerned about the vacation. That is a trivial matter: I did not come to China to eat ice cream at the seaside. I am concerned about the way the decision has been made, about how all these decisions are made. I came to China to learn…"

"We are happy to help him. If he had not questioned his contract, it would still be October. Bei Dai He is very nice in October…"

"It does not say Bei Dai He in my contract. Not the one I signed: it says 'visits to Chinese cities' and on the copy I signed I wrote in the names Yenan, Chingkanshan, Hunan…"

"We never received that copy of his contract."

"But I gave it to Comrade Yen Wei."

"She forgot to give it to us. She has been reprimanded."

Now, where I come from, industrial disputes, disagreements like this about contracts are settled by arbitration and, if that fails, by a strike:

"I am offering to give up my vacation and stay behind and work on the new textbook. If, instead, you now force me to go on holiday at the seaside against my wishes, I will have no option but to go on strike."

The interpreter pauses, looks up, unsure if he's heard right. I translate it for him:

"Pa Gong."

It sounds like a grenade exploding - or only a thunder clap out of Chinese opera because, well: there is no right to strike in China.

Yen Wei is sent to talk to me: "Some years ago, a foreign friend, Mr. Reichenbach, was sent to prison. It was just after the end of the Cultural Revolution. He was accused of practicing an ultra-leftist, Trotskyist, anarchist line. It is a very serious crime. .He is still there…"

We have gone out to Peking University to see the wall posters. Jiang Qing's protégés at The People's Daily have announced a new Big Character Poster campaign - Cultural Revolution tactics, although this time everyone has been told exactly what to write. If

Yen Wei has red eyes it's because all the students have been staying up all night copying the words down and then parading them to ready-made walls and pasting them up. They are all directed against Deng Xiao-ping, Mao's designated successor, known popularly as Mr. Cat-and-Mouse. It's a dangerous profession, being Mao's successor - every previous one has been purged: Lin Piao who died in a plane crash trying, it is said, to escape to Russia; Liu Shao-chi, who was tortured in public, his teeth knocked out, medicines withheld: he had to be fed through a tube in his nose and died naked on a cement floor in a provincial prison. His wife and children were made to watch.

The wall posters record a steady escalation of epithets: beginning as a "Capitalist-roader," Deng has become a "Poisonous revisionist," then a "Frenzied backslider," "A mad dog barking at the sun," and now "A stinking piece of bean-curd…"

I say:

"Is a piece of stinking bean-curd worse than a turtle's egg?"

"A turtle's egg is not as bad as a rotten egg. He can still be reformed. It is only when it says that he is beyond reform that his position becomes really serious."

"Is Deng Xiao-ping beyond reform?"

"His mistakes have been pointed out to him. It is now up to him."

"And if he persists?"

"Then he becomes an Enemy of the People, an Enemy of the Party…" and then she turns to me and says:

"Da Wei Boshi…"

Woops, we're using titles:

"Dr. David: you must not underestimate the danger of what you are doing. Mr. Reichenbach did. What will your wife and children do during the six years he has been in prison?"

You can say that better in Chinese: "What will they do during the Mr-Reichenbach-in-prison-kind-of-six-years?"

II

Ed did expect an invitation to Mao's Victory Parade. Of course he did: I mean, it was his party too. Wasn't it? Back in America, he waited impatiently for the mailman, wondered what presents to take, contacted Rewi Alley, Mme. Soong, even wrote to The Man himself, wondering "why I've never received any reply to my letters, even though I have been assured you received them?"

In the end, like a jilted lover, he read the announcement in the newspapers.

Of course he was disappointed, but he did what all Friends of China do and would go on doing: he made their excuses for them. They were, he told himself, too busy getting on with the revolution to have any time for sentimental reunions. He was philosophical: "When you're lucky enough to reach the age of reflection, you know that a long life is not measured in years but in the number of lives you live." He didn't mean that in any Buddhist or Hindu sense: there were new adventures waiting for him out there, weren't there, new loves, new roles: he was sure of it...?

Ed was not a man of the theatre and it took him some time to realize that, in fact, he was like an actor who has played a role too well and could no longer ever be separated from it. His fame was an iron mask, a jeweled scorpion, a squirrel's cage. He would always be "that Red Star-guy," "Mao's Man." It took him some time to find out that the role he'd written for himself was in a tragedy.

Not that he was short of other contacts with other men of note: Nehru, Gandhi, Prince Saud, FDR, Truman... But all Nehru taught him was how to stand on his head, and he watched, horrified, as Gandhi's funeral turned into a riot when armed Gurkhas beat back a crowd of two million who threatened to crush the funeral pyre of the guru of non-violence. So much for that option, he growled. In Russia, Stalin wouldn't even receive him. At first Ed tried to bribe the man they called The Goon and who was in charge of the foreign press corps by giving him his chocolate ration and, when that didn't work, presented him with a large box of laxatives disguised as chocolate drops. In the end, he spent his time in Moscow having an affair with a University student "with azure eyes" and supervising the fair distribution of peanut butter to American correspondents at the American Embassy.

He interviewed Goering when he was captured, was the first reporter to enter liberated Vienna, crashed his car in Paris and then sold the wreck to pay off his debts at poker. He was in Prague when the Russians marched in and crushed the last democratic government in Eastern Europe. No-one listened when Ed warned that the Russians would never leave.

As for his fellow-Americans: when he'd first arrived home, Robert Taft, Mr. Republican himself, told him that "it is fantastic to suppose there is any danger of attack on the United States by Japan."

Herbert Hoover agreed, and so did John Foster Dulles: "Only hysteria entertains the idea that Germany, Japan or Italy contemplates war on us."

In 1941, Ernest Hemingway visited China and wrote that Ed had exaggerated the Reds' importance.

The only people who seemed to have learned anything from Red Star were the guerrillas in the Philippines, Burma, Malaysia and Vietnam - where Ed watched the French use the Japanese troops who had surrendered to them to put down the Vietnamese freedom fighters.

Red Star even cost him his marriage. Ed was very gentlemanly about it, would say nothing bad about Peg in his autobiography, quoting Shaw that "all autobiographies are lies: no man is bad enough to tell the truth about himself during his lifetime, or about his family and friends." But everyone knew Peg had a bad case of what the Chinese call "red-eye disease:" bleeding with jealousy, humiliated at living in Ed's shadow. She was "Mao's Man's Wife - yes, I think she writes too: same sort of stuff, but not as good."

But that, according to Peg, was because Ed had the mornings to write while she had to busy herself organizing the servants, choosing which dress to wear to the next party, designing her own table napkins. Ed tried to make the marriage work, helping Peg get to Sian so she could cover Chiang's kidnapping, sending her a package of rat traps when she complained about the nightly invasion of her cave. If he couldn't have another woman, he could at least help the one he had become more of a real companion. And for a while it worked, Peg very enthusiastic about Indusco, and not at all impressed by Mao who, she said, wouldn't even be able to improve the way servants were hired. Though Ed wanted to believe she could be a good writer, Peg's real talent was organizing other people to do the things she herself could never do, remind them of ideals, cocooned as she herself was from ever having to face the mess of translating them into reality. Indusco suited her, not least appealing to her strident pro-Americanism: Americans were the most advanced species of human beings, excelling in generosity, kindness, friendliness: "I would not give up the American people for all the Parthenons, all the Beethoven symphonies, all the English literature, all the French cuisine, all the Taj Mahals, and all the Russian and Chinese revolutions, all combined." Her opposition to the British Empire was not that it was wrong, but that America should always be number one, never number two.

Ed could sympathize with none of this, and so the distance between them only grew wider. It was a bitter divorce, Peg arguing that he had ruined her life and taking him to the cleaners, attaching all his royalties and earnings: "You never loved me and I, I never loved you. I loved who I thought you were..."

Ed ate himself away with remorse and guilt: "What a complete skunk I've been."

Because he'd met someone else - an actress. Yes, he too.

He followed events in China from a distance, a bit surprised that there was so little news about the person he'd already recognized as his successor. Mao had told him that, as a condition of being allowed to marry him, Jiang Qing had promised she would play no role at all in politics. Ed understood: the cruelest men in China's history have been her Empresses - and their eunuchs. He understood that her Yang side had to be castrated, but suspected it would only make her add revenge to envy - a dangerous combination.

What really upset him about the news that did trickle out of China was the way she was turning so anti-American:

"It could have been avoided," he told friends: "it doesn't need to happen, goddammit." Why did they have to send Hurley to Peking, in his cowboy hat: "He's the only man I ever met who can strut sitting down." He couldn't even pronounce Mao's name, calling him Mouse Tongue or Mouse Dung. "Mao was never anti-American," Ed wrote: "he was made anti-American by the treatment he received: did you know he offered in 1945 to go to the States himself?" When Colonel Barrett was sent to tell him the answer was no, Mao flew into a rage:

"If you Americans, sated with bread and sleep, want to curse the people and back Chiang, that's your business. Back him as long as you want. But remember one thing. China is whose China? It sure as hell is not Chiang Kai-shek's: it belongs to the Chinese people!"

America snubbed Mao, but you don't snub a man like that and then turn your back on him…

If supporting Mao could have prevented Pearl Harbor, dropping Chiang could have prevented Korea: "that's a lot of blood on someone's hands."

It made it all seem so sad, but it is the tragedy of Cassandras that they can only stand in the shadows and watch as their predictions come true:

"What's more, some of them would never forgive us for having prematurely spoken the harsh truth."

One such was a Senator looking for a scoop: in 1953, two agents turned up at Ed's house. They already had a voluminous file on him and reported that "Mr. Snow states categorically that he has never been a Communist, is not a Communist, will never be a Communist." He was, they reported, cordial, cooperative and "apparently" frank. But so are all spies: McCarthy was soon accusing Ed of being "the chief propagandist for Communism," and "selling China to the Russians."

"China never was ours to sell!" Ed fumed.

No-one leapt to his defense: he had been a friend of China, and so, therefore, to have been his friend or even to possess a copy of Ed's book was itself evidence of Communist sympathies. Though never formally charged with anything, his books were burned in US libraries in Europe.

His new wife was blacklisted on Broadway.

Desperate for money, he wrote a couple of travel pieces - on Flagstaff and Acapulco, tried to write short stories but no-one would publish them. He resigned from The Post, tried to retire, live the life of a paterfamilias, dandling his two young children on his knee and pottering in the garden. He bought some sheep to eat the grass so as to save himself the trouble of mowing the lawn, but was irritated when they ate everything else too, including the fruit trees.

Ed had reached the line: the one where you begin to look back more often and more fondly than forward, the line where you know that the past is now going to grow more and more precious as the future grows less and less inviting.

He began to read the Romantic poets - Keats, Shelley, Byron: he understood them now but felt closer to T.S. Eliot, lines from The Hollow Men whispering like rats' feet over broken glass in his dry brain:

"At the hour when we are
Trembling with tenderness
Lips that would kiss
Form prayers to broken stone."

He began to understand why there is an exceptionally high suicide rate among journalists.

Eventually he surrendered to his fate: if he would always and only be "Mao's Man," then it was time to come out with the sequel - a new book: China After the Revolution. He didn't expect it to be so upbeat as Red Star:

"Then I had just discovered that Evil exists in the world," he told his publisher, "and then I believed that people were capable of destroying it fairly swiftly. Now I know that quick remedies often perpetuate or worsen Evil or only give it a new form..."

He'd heard about the Hundred Flowers campaign and that Mao was planning another such "quick remedy" and wanted to be there when it happened.

And then, as the "wasted decade of the Fifties" drew to its close, the wind suddenly changed: China was divorcing the Russians and flirting with a new relationship with America: he, Ed, would once again be the marriage broker, the message-bearer... The only problem was that the US didn't recognize China - it didn't exist: "There are no planes to Peking."

It took another year of negotiations, but eventually a Machiavellian solution was found: the US would grant him a passport to visit China only if he went as an accredited correspondent; China would only let him in as a private individual: "Officially I entered China as a-writer-not-a-correspondent while in Washington I entered as a-correspondent-not-a-writer."

He expected to pay his way with the royalties from the Chinese edition of Red Star and was disappointed to find that there weren't any: it too didn't exist.

He flew into Peking in late June and was taken on a long detour through Manchuria, Sian, Yenan, down to Shanghai and across to Szechuan and Yunnan. Everywhere he had an official guide who heavily restricted his movements: "Hell," he fumed, "I had more freedom of movement in Chiang's China than now." Everywhere he met people he'd known before: "then in their youth, ragged, hungry, so-called bandits, now the equivalents of account-executives, managers, chairmen of boards, big shots."

They took him to see a model commune - Nanjie, and eventually to the "Very High Official" at the top. As he stood with Mao on the rostrum and looked down at the square, at a million people in identical blue cotton suits and caps, he wondered if she was there. His spectacles had broken, one of the arms had come apart from the frame: he took them off and fixed it with the elastic band he always wore on his wrist. It made the spectacles sit a bit awry on his nose, the vision somewhat blurred.

Afterwards they retired to the Small Palace of the Fragrant Concubine. The Chairman himself was a bit of a shock: he had grown as fat as a sea elephant, only the hands still delicate. His face was moonlike, the eyes difficult to read. He was in the early stages of Parkinson's disease and nurses hovered on the edges. His fingers were stained yellow and his teeth blackened from chain-smoking.

Through the windows Ed could see snarling bronze dragons and a swimming pool; in the distance a lake.

The conversation over lunch was desultory at first: Mao didn't know that Ed was divorced and had remarried, referred to Rewi Alley as an Australian and didn't know that George Hatem had eradicated syphilis from China. There was some catching up to do. He claimed great success for the Great Leap Forward and when Ed said he'd heard reports of starvation, Mao replied that austerity is good for people, for their revolutionary character, and offered Ed a toothpick: "Here, have two more for your children: you can say Mao Zedong gives them to you." When Ed pressed him about the Great Leap Forward, Mao suddenly got to his feet, gestured to Ed to follow him, and led him out through the French windows into the garden.

The courtyard was dominated by a brand-new, Olympic-size swimming pool: glassed in and heated so the Chairman could swim all year round. Mao stripped down to his trunks and belly-flopped in the water, beckoning Ed to join him. But Ed hadn't come to China to go swimming. The garden backed onto a wall with large windows and French doors, through which Ed could see into the Chairman's bedroom: a king-size bed, fluffed with many pillows and scattered with half-read books which spilled over onto the apple-green carpet. Ed had already heard the rumors about the books and the bed:

"The books are procured for him by Kang Sheng," they whispered to him: "Jiang Qing's sidekick. Mao is said to have the greatest collection of erotica in China."

Ed just shrugged: that's not so unusual: all the Chinese Emperors collected such pillow-books, the greatest of them all - "The Golden Lotus" - written on sheets of fine rice paper with a camel's hair brush - which, as well as the ink, dripped a pinpoint of poison on each page. The drops caused the pages to stick together, so the reader had to moisten a finger with his tongue: it is said that the first reader fell dead as he turned the last page.

And Kang Sheng didn't only bring him books, he brought him girls too, young virgins who cavorted naked in the swimming pool before retiring to this bedroom where Mao would feed on their juices - the classic Chinese formula for longevity.

It was said that Jiang Qing lived on the other side of the courtyard - in the Garden of Stillness - but when Ed was there only a frog hopped along the path joining the two.

Mao hauled his blubbery body out of the pool and, dripping wet, led Ed through the French doors into the bedroom. As he dressed, Ed noticed the Encyclopaedia Britannica lying open on a desk: evidence of Mao's latest attack on the English language. On the desk was a magnifying glass and next to it a spittoon.

Mao lit a cigarette, held the long wooden match between his fingers, watching the flame burn down. Then he snuffed it out and leaned forward:

"I have been betrayed," he said simply: "During the Hundred Flowers campaign we dug up all sorts of people who were planning to overthrow the government." They had been given plenty of time to expose themselves "but the real traitor is still at large" - hiding among the disciples. "They lied to me about the successes of the Great Leap Forward."

He looked up, asked Ed not to take notes, and when Ed put his pen away, continued:

"There are people in positions of power - in the highest echelons - who think China should now take the capitalist road. Once they are out in the open..." He paused: "We must boldly unleash the masses: we must not be like women with bound feet. We need determined people, young, with little education, untainted by the old ways: people with little learning but much truth."

He stopped then and when Ed tried to break the awkward silence by asking him about his private life, his wife, Mao at first frowned: "Settle for the biography you already published," he said: "Better not write my story any more: developments in the future will be a hard thing to write about."

But then he dismissed the nurse curtly and, when she'd gone, blurted it all out:

"Only Jiang Qing completely supports me," he said, "when everyone else let me down, she came to me."

Ed said nothing, desperately trying to commit as much as possible to memory, to get as much as possible verbatim.

So they had had their autumn love-affair...?

"She didn't even say 'what took you so long?" said Mao, wonderingly: "She has moved back in - over there," he pointed across the garden. "She told me how she used to cry when they sabotaged everything I tried to do, when they cornered me, forced Deng on me to clean things up. Things don't need cleaning up, they need stirring up! Fuck their mother's cunt: how dare they forget they owe everything to me."

But she's got it all worked out, he said: the cast, the villains, the plot, the Superhero...

Ed's emotions were jangling, he was anxious to get away, to get to his typewriter, but Mao was, once again, one step ahead of him:

"I haven't told you any of this, all right? Friend..."

Ed nodded, asked - lamely, hopefully:

"Is there anything you do want me to tell the American people, the American government?" Mao shook his head, then smiled:

"If I do, I'll call you. I always do, don't I?"

So when they asked him back home if he had anything worth publishing from the visit, all Ed said was that he was working on a short story.

If he couldn't write history any more, he could still edit stories.

They're not that different, are they?

How The Swallow Lost Its Tail: Part Two

On October first, 1949, I stood in Tienanmen as a captured Sherman tank escorted Chairman Mao's car to the Imperial Palace, and loudspeaker vans congratulated the people of Peking on their liberation. Then he appeared, in a new suit, on the balcony above the Gate of Heavenly Peace. We were lined up in the square, organized in position by numbers written on the flagstones.

"The Chinese people have stood up," Chairman Mao called out to us: "nobody will ever insult us ever again."

But then:

"We must now put aside the things we know well and be compelled to do things we don't know well."

Lao Kou and I were sent to the wilderness, to Nanniwan, a wasteland thirty-five miles southeast of Yenan where we were to create a productive village out of nothing. They gave us just enough seed grain for one season: if it failed, we would die.

We gouged cave dwellings out of the hills, made clothes from the hair of black mountain goats, melted down the metal in the old temple to make farm tools, made paper out of birchbark... A year later, I gave birth to a daughter, and in January 1951, Lao Kou pulled the necessary strings for us to be sent to build a model village in Nanjie. There we would supervise the transition to socialism, and create something visitors could be brought to see. Lao Kou had hoped to be sent to Peking; I didn't. I am just a simple Chinese woman caught up in a time of great change who wanted to play her small part. The new society we dreamed of would not be created in Peking, or Shanghai: if it was going to happen, it had to happen in ten thousand Nanjies. Or it would not happen at all...

It was not a rich village, too far from any major town to provide a ready supply of urban night soil or a market for the vegetables and tobacco the peasants grew on their private plots. It had no shops, just a little store, which sold soap, matches, candles and needles -

the only things the peasants needed which they couldn't make for themselves.

The peasants welcomed us, though they didn't really believe us: they took the land when we gave it to them, took their revenge on the landlords who had persecuted them, but everyone in the past had cheated them and they were waiting to see how we were going to do it to them. We Chinese have always believed that our gods grant us special favors if we kow-tow to them long enough, and they sensed immediately who the new gods were.

Fortunately we had a ready-made enemy to direct their anger against. Nanjie was a village like many others, except that it already had a co-operative. It had been established by an organization called Indusco, the brainchild of an American journalist and his wife - in collaboration with at least one imperialist government and the Kuomintang. We saw it at once for what it was: part of a counter-revolutionary plot to bypass the revolution. If they couldn't defeat us on the battlefield, they would destroy us by adding a thin layer of socialism to disguise the capitalist base

It was radish tactics - red on the outside, white on the inside.

The man in charge of it was nice enough: a New Zealander, named Rewi Alley. He had flaming red hair and a nose like a hawk, but he was actually a gentle man who had adopted two Chinese children, famine orphans. He probably meant well; they all probably meant well, but they were trying to steal our revolution.

We put up wall posters denouncing him: the peasants came and read them and then went back to their houses, played chess or cards, mended tools, wove baskets, mashed wood pulp so we could make more paper. The foreign devil called a public meeting to reply to our accusations. The peasants came with their pipes and half-woven baskets and children, sat on little three-legged stools in the open air outside the old pagoda, and listened as the foreign devil told them how well they were doing, that there would be a bonus this year. Then Lao Kou stood up, pointed his finger at the foreign devil, accused him of using sugar-coated bullets, and then asked if everyone in the village got the same income?

No.

"So there are inequalities?"

Of course, they said: some men are stronger than others, have larger families: they can work harder, so they earn more. It has always been that way: it's natural.

"But don't you see that this only creates jealousy, envy, unhappiness?"

One burly peasant with a shaved head and bristly chin stood up and said:

"If everyone got the same wage, the strong would only work as hard as the weak."

Lao Kou looked at him:

"You are a strong man."

The man grinned: yes.

"Should you therefore live better than your neighbors - just because of some accident of birth?"

"What accident of birth?" the peasant wanted to know, indignantly: "there was no accident..."

"No, what I mean is this," explained Lao Kou patiently: "The bourgeoisie says that man is basically a selfish, frightened creature - and until now they were right, because until now there never was a system in which men did not have to be selfish and frightened. But now there is: you do not need to be selfish any more because everyone will be guaranteed food, shelter, a decent burial. All you have to do is give up fear."

The burly peasant wanted to know who said he was afraid of anyone, and Lao Kou said:

"I do: you are afraid of change. You talk blind talk, see only the garlic skin. Just because it's never happened before..."

The next day he closed the co-operative down and told the foreign devil to get out - and quick, before he took his children away from him.

"Belief takes time," he said: "Obedience is quicker. It takes time to convert people but to make them obey, all you have to do is frighten them."

I knew he was right and I knew he was wrong: with their obedience we could build a socialist economy, but if we had only their obedience, we would lose their minds. I was afraid that's why they obeyed: to keep their minds to themselves. But Lao Kou said he didn't care about their minds; he was learning the new rules fast and was soon transferred to the capital. I stayed behind: there was much to do: an order for wheelbarrows so that people could transport the sick to hospital; a campaign against cockroaches which were to be killed by soaking a piece of cotton in DDT, putting it in a bottle cap and placing the cap under the bed.

Dozens of tiny details which make up real life.

We were living socialism; soon we would be proper Communists. We might not live to see it, but our children would - all our children. There were enough orphans to keep us busy: to set an example, I had myself sterilized. I didn't want the life of an ordinary wife and mother. Not when there was a great cause to carry out.

We could have made it. But then America began the Korean War, fearing our alternative might infect the whole world. We dug air-raid shelters and built dormitories to house the refugees who would soon stream out of the cities when America dropped atomic bombs and biological weapons on us. As soon as we had defeated the Americans, the Russians would be next: all former friends were now potential enemies - especially foreigners who have developed their long noses from poking holes in our windows, and round eyes from what they saw there. The Party launched the Hundred Flowers campaign to draw out all the cockroaches and termites, the rotten eggs and backsliders and expose them. The weeds had to be uprooted, and even flowers steal an unfair share of the sun.

None of this caused much disturbance in Nanjie Village: we were too busy planting and sewing and reaping. We had a quota to fill and Lao Kou made sure that we always did. It wasn't lying: Communists don't lie. But we Chinese do prefer to avoid speaking bad luck things, and have always told our Emperors what they wanted to hear.

Then came the Great Leap Forward: China was going to jump

straight into Communism. I put up notices: all private property is confiscated - land, pigs, chickens, even shovels and hoes. All private houses were torn down and the rubble used to build communal dormitories - one for men, another for women, and a crèche for the children who would be brought up collectively. Everyone was given free clothes - blue tunics and trousers - men and women alike; everyone ate in the common mess hall from a common rice bowl.

There was no cash: it was not necessary.

We could have made it work. We would never have become rich, but we could have made it a happy place, a place where you could feel you belonged. But Peking then ordered us to set up a steel mill: China was to match England in steel production in fifteen years, so we gathered together everything made of metal and smelted it down in backyard furnaces. We had no iron ore but we had picks, shovels, hoes, rakes, axes, hammers, pitchforks. When the peasants complained and hid things, I told them we could tend the land with our bare hands and sharp sticks. Tin roofs, nails, bolts, hinges, locks, even small tractors were thrown in the furnace and melted down.

We were so thorough that we ran out of charcoal for the furnace. So we went out and cut down every tree: fruit trees, shade trees. It caused serious erosion but we had no time now to plant or bring in the harvest in any case. We were told that the new commune system was so successful that there was plenty of food for all.

By 1959, we were living on a grain allocation of 125 grams per day: enough for one small cup of rice and two thin slices of bread.

Some of the men organized a strike then, refusing to work until they were fed, or at least given a proper explanation. I tried talking to them, but when Lao Kou heard about it, he sent down a squad of PLA soldiers whose bayonets forced them back in line, the ringleaders taken away and never heard of again.

People began to die - slowly, using up their fat reserves until they were walking skeletons. There was no bark or leaves to supplement the diet: there were no trees any more. Lao Kou came down with an inspection team, which wanted to see for themselves how much grain we really had in our granary. The team leader picked up a bamboo pole and stabbed it into the heap: the thin layer of rice trickled to one side and exposed the mound of straw Lao Kou had ordered placed underneath to make it look bigger than it was.

I expected him to be criticized, but the team leader just looked at it, smiled and said:

"I see your rice has very long straws."

I don't know how many people died - some say five million, ten: in our village, no babies were born for three years.

And then, suddenly, we were told - not that it had all been a mistake, but that there was another way. We were instructed to reintroduce profit incentives, allocate the peasants private lots, allow private markets. When we said "But that's capitalism," they replied that economic policy was now under the control of Deng Xiao-ping whose new slogan was: "It doesn't matter whether the cat is black or white so long as it catches the mouse."

We didn't ask what mouse; we didn't ask any questions any more.

During this time, Lao Kou and I had drifted apart. I would have left him, but the new marriage law made divorce much more difficult than before - virtually impossible for anyone whose husband had been a soldier in the anti-Japanese War. He had got our daughter into a special school in Peking, reserved for the children of cadres and bureaucrats: Lao Kou was rising fast - in the process widening the gap between us. Down here, they know a way of poisoning the body, which leaves no trace: they strip the hairs off certain kinds of bamboo, or certain caterpillars: their hairs have sharp tips, and they are barbed, like fish hooks. Put them in someone's drink: they have no taste, no smell. As they slip down the intestines, they tear them to pieces: that, I feared when I looked at Lao Kou and those like him, was how China, my China, was going to die, eaten away from within.

One day I went up to Peking to see my daughter. She was excited, had been selected to march in the great parade celebrating the anniversary of Liberation. I stood in Tienanmen, but couldn't see her for the crowds. Up on the balcony stood the Chairman; near him, in the background, a silver-haired white man. After the parade, I asked my daughter if she knew who he was?

"Oh, an old friend of the Chairman - from the old days. A caveman."

When I asked her how she knew that, she took me by the hand, led me to Chongnanhai where all the Party leaders lived, then down a side alley to a small door where she showed the guard a pass and led us through.

This had once been the Forbidden City: beyond the gate lay a fairyland of lakes and parks and palaces. Fresh snow glistened pink in the setting sun.

She pointed:

"There, the Garden of Abundance. In the old days, every spring, the emperor performed the sowing rites there to ensure an abundant harvest. Chairman Mao lives over there..."

She pointed and laughed:

"It used to be called the Hall of Friendly Talks, now it's been renamed The Hall of Longevity."

"Then he will live for ever?"

She smiled, pointed: "Look, the Small Palace of the Fragrant Concubine."

I could smell the jasmine on the breeze. The yellow tiles on the roof ended in swallow wings. I could hear the magpies calling and the cranes from the lake.

"That's where the Chairman has his offices," she said, and then laughed again:

"But he does most of his work in bed."

I stopped, looked at her; she looked back at me and then dropped her eyes.

I never asked her how she knew all this, or how she got the pass. I had known for some time that to find my place in this world, I would have to change it all. But this was not my world. And if nothing was done soon, it never would be...

December 1975, Peking

There is a little red bridge in Purple Bamboo Park, a narrow wooden bridge with a low balustrade. The water is polluted with fine black dust from the new coal-brick factory on the other side of the river, but men still fish in it and boys float paper boats down it.

Couples lean on the wooden railing and watch their faces flicker and merge as in a kiss, for water is shameless.

Yen Wei has arranged to meet me here. As I wait for her, I watch an old man with a bamboo rod catch tiddlers and then throw them back in, after holding them up between forefinger and thumb, silver bodies flashing for an instant in his eyes.

And then she's there, leaning on the railing next to me.

I say:

"The lotus leaves are lovely like that, don't you think, the edges curled? They look like big ear-trumpets. Do you suppose the fish listen to us, too?"

She looks quickly round, her nervousness like an electric spark between us.

I say:

"Do you know what happened when the fish married a grasshopper?"

She looks at me, baffled; I say:

"It's a game Tracey and I play: the answer is a frog…"

"Frogs hibernate in winter," she replies: "They bury themselves in the mud, waiting for the spring…"

She looks round again: no microphones in the trees, only loudspeakers blaring revolutionary songs, the words barely recognizable between the scratches and cracks.

"I have a message for you. From the leadership. They say now that now you are on strike, and so have no income, your wife and children may have to be deported."

"I see. And me?"

"You stay…"

"Ah."

"...for the full two years of your contract."

"Ah."

"Two working years..."

"I see."

"That is the message the leadership asked me to deliver to you. I must return with Da Wei's answer."

"I will talk it over with my wife and children..."

I look down at the river: frogs have big ears, but they're all asleep, aren't they?

"When will he have his answer?"

"Oh, about a week. Shall we meet here again - in a week's time?"

She nods:

"I am sorry it has come to this... I think you mean well. It should not be like this..."

No.

I watch her walk away, eyes down, shoulders hunched, pigtails tucked under her cap: it takes courage to do what she has just done, effort. The China-bashers say that all the Cultural Revolution achieved was turn a whole people into compliant puppets, but puppets don't have hearts, feelings. So they can't be torn apart by the terrible conflicts people go through when they have to swallow down their personal feelings - not to mention friendliness, truth - because they still believe in a system, have to believe in it: they've given their lives to it. Friendship, personal feelings, truth are all "bourgeois," of course, but you may as well call them "heretical" or "infidel" or "unamerican."

Revolutions have only one failing: they turn in circles, getting ever smaller until they implode on their own momentum.

Leaving only nostalgia behind.

The whiff of it in the breeze.

It is clear to me as I stand on that little red bridge that my reason for coming to China - to live the next Cultural Revolution - is not going to happen. And from what I've seen, I don't mind. You can't force-feed people revolution: they're not Peking ducks. You can't herd people or drag people into the future: all you achieve is the caution that camouflages fear, the evasion that diverts challenge, the compliance that substitutes for belief.

But I have come to love these people nevertheless and it is ironic that it should have been while I was on strike and ready to leave that I found reason to want to stay.

For five or six weeks, we just went out and looked - at what's really there. It wasn't what we'd hoped to find, not what they said it would be like; it was something else: a quiet dignity, a stoic courage, a determination to survive and the knowledge that you can. After the Cultural Revolution everyone knew they were vulnerable, that the world is a fragile place. If the President of the Republic, the Secretary General of the Communist Party, the Chief of Staff of the Army, the mayors of Peking, Shanghai, half the Central Committee and even the author of 'The East is Red' could all be pulled out, made to pass the gate, no-one was safe. But, in the midst of that trembling fragility and stalking terror, people found something else - that there is always a place deep down where you can go and renew your contract with yourself.

Frogs have this special ability to change color and disappear into their surroundings. It may not be as much fun as hopping around on lotus leaves, but at least it's safe and warm down there in the thick rich mud. Those that get caught are taken away to be dissected by eager children.

Each morning, we dress Tracey and Jessica in five layers of clothes, put them snug in the sidecar and cycle out down all the wide avenues and narrow back-alleys, along straight canals and twisting backwaters, past the frozen fields, the mud-walled villages.

It is so cold the carters no longer sleep on their carts but race their horses along the roads, manes and fur-hats flying, tails and whips lashing, mouths and teeth gasping at the cold air. I wonder if the thaw will ever come.

We find wonderful little restaurants out in the communes around Peking where we can buy dumplings steamed over pine needles and hot bread baked with red chillies. Muslim restaurants where they wear little white skull-caps and long embroidered skirts, drink a lot and are boisterous in a way the Han never are in public. Afterwards we stroll replete down the village street: children skip over long rubber bands and spin tops. Old men lean against a sunny wall, chatting toothlessly, long thin pipes between their pink gums, sucking a few puffs from thimble-sized bowls. I know that smell: the Chinese use marijuana seeds for medicine, calling it Huo Ma, Fire Hemp, but have no use for the flowers. Such then is the reward for the end of a busy life: to sit in the sun and get stoned...

We can't go very far: at the fifteen kilometre post, there are guards with fixed bayonets and reflecting sunglasses, who stop us, ask for our permits; we look wistfully at the long road winding up into the hills, turn round and cycle back.

We see more of Peking in these five weeks in limbo than we ever would in two years of Sunday outings. Limbo, of course, is where those who died before Christ's Coming were sent - and those who doubt there will be a Second Coming. We cycle out to see the Sleeping Buddha in the Temple of Awakening, for some say he is only asleep. In the Temple of the Azure Clouds, there are five hundred statues of the Buddha of the Future, each with a different face: one of them shows an old man tearing the skin away from the young face underneath. They are out near the Summer Palace; the huge lake is frozen over now: they say it flows all the way into Chongnanhai... We hire skates and make a skateboard for Tracey by screwing a pair of blades on the bottom of the lid of one of packing cases we brought our things in. She sits on it and I skate out along the ice, pull her round and round in a circle, her long hair flying out from under her fur hat, teeth laughing into the wind.

Afterwards we buy little sticks of red, toffee-coated crab-apples for the children: they look as if their red cheeks have been sliced off for them to eat.

Tracey says:

"When Mummy grows old will she look like a Chinese lady?"

"No: she'll look like Nana."

"I like Nana. When Nana grows old will she look like a Chinese lady?"

"No: Nana's European."

"What's European mean?"

"People with blotchy pink skin."

"Good job I don't have blotchy pink skin."

She's worked it out: "Chinese" means her creamy skin, her leaf-shaped eyes, her raven-black hair. The rest is what you make of it. She loves going to the old Summer Palace and it is a sadly beautiful place: rice fields now cover what was once The Garden of Eternal Spring and The Garden of Eternity - a good place to remember that no Spring lasts for ever and no government for Eternity, only people...

Back home, we have a family discussion to decide what to do about Yen Wei's message. The British Consul was blunt and to-the-point:

"You are here as a private individual. Which means you're entitled to an invitation to Christmas luncheon and the Queens' birthday and you can use the Library. Beyond that, we're not sure what you're up to here... You've never registered..."

"I didn't want to have any contact with you. Nothing personal. I thought it would compromise me with the Chinese, make them suspicious."

"Well," he said: "we all make our bed and must lie in it," and then: "How could you do it? How could you trust them, how could you be so naïve? You know what these people did to Donald Grey's cat, don't you?"

"Donald who?"

"The British consul, my predecessor. In the Cultural Revolution, they cornered him in a tiny room, kept him locked up there for eight weeks, his only company his cat - which they strangled and hanged from the light flex. I mean: how could you ever trust people who'd do a thing like that?"

"Is he still here - Donald Grey?"

"No. He made a lot of money out of a book he wrote about it all. Called it 'No Room To Swing a Cat' - no, that's a joke: bad taste."

He got up, extended a languid hand:

"I suppose if the worst comes to the worst, we can get your wife and children out for you... I'm not sure about your daughter though: she's Chinese, isn't she? You may have to give her back..."

That evening, at the Friendship Guesthouse, we go in to dinner and everyone looks away. It's startling, the synchronized gesture... Tracey's best friend, Lucy, is not there, so we go over to the table occupied by the Austrians:

"Hello, good evening, may we join you?"

Elizabeth nods at her husband, they get up and leave. I look over at Harry and Susan, two American Baptists who've been here for thirty years. Harry shrugs, gives a sheepish smile and looks away; Susan is very busy with her chopsticks.

After dinner, Ken comes to see us. He stands in the doorway:

"You've been sent to Coventry, old mate. We've all been told you're too dangerous to talk to, to be seen talking to. That you're under investigation."

"Oh... Do you want to come in?"

But he just grimaces and turns away; I say:

"Thanks for telling us..."

He grunts, leaves, I close the door.

What shall we do?

If I were Chinese I'd know what to do.

They have invented not one but two philosophies to live by. They are both Confucian and Taoist at the same time: Confucian in their public compliance, Taoist in private:

"Bend and be straight...

If you are courageous in daring you will die.

If you are courageous in not-daring you will live."

III

Ed was back again in 1964 - still hoping. Chou En-lai gave him a warm coat but otherwise all he got was another exhausting tour of everything they wanted him to see. There were vague hints about a possible message: China was at ideological war with Russia - MaoZedong-Thought versus Goulash-Communism. The Russians held Ed responsible for it, for the whole split in the world Communist movement: Red Star had been the first the world had heard of Mao; Ed was an American, therefore it was obvious: Maoism was part of a plot by America to divide and rule the world.

What was true was that China did seek a rapprochement with America - building bridges, they called it; Vietnam and the Cultural Revolution put that on the back burner but by 1970, China was ready to send a message.

Ed was summoned back to Peking.

He had followed the course of the Cultural Revolution with a mixture of intense excitement and moral repulsion, excitement because of the daring of it - to call on a whole nation, a whole people and especially its young to rise up and clean out their own government; repulsion because of the personality cult, the strident self-righteousness, the waste.

"Mao has become impatient," he said to himself as he mowed the lawn: "He needs enemies like a cat needs mice and if he can't find any, he has to invent some."

Former colleagues, old partners, old friends...

"Yes," he argued with himself as he pulled out the weeds: "of course, it's about power too, it's about revenge: yes, of course, innocent people get hurt, die, but it's also about keeping the revolution alive. And that's a problem, isn't it, because the only thing people can revolt against after the revolution is...? Revolution itself...?"

He never saw it first-hand, but his heirs did - Strong, Robinson,

188

Hinton. Ed felt ambivalent about them too, the new China-hacks, earning their right to live in China by endlessly polishing the stars, Ed noting caustically that Hinton had used the fortune he'd made out his books on the commune system to buy a farm in Pennsylvania - which he ran single-handed. He knew them all, suspected that if he'd been born a generation later, he'd probably be one of them. They were only doing what he had done: attempting to combine reporting the truth with a committed involvement, which made them - like him - leave some things out. He tried to justify himself by saying things like "If you can't take the heat, don't go in the kitchen," "You can't make an omelette without breaking eggs" or "Who are you that your shit don't stink?" But he knew deep down that the heat burned a hole in his conscience too, that one rotten egg can spoil even the best omelette, and that Jesus didn't shit - or so Ed's Mum had told him when he was a kid back in Missouri.

What he feared most was that China was not just tearing itself apart but leaving itself vulnerable to attack: Chiang stood on the cliffs of Taiwan, poised to invade. Ed understood when the Army put an end to the Cultural Revolution, noting that at the Ninth Congress of the Party in 1969, 90 of the 170 places on the Central Committee went to Army men, and 13 of the 25 members of the Politburo.

"What must the true believers be feeling?" he wondered as he burned the dead leaves of autumn: "those who did everything Mao asked of them, only to find themselves now digging ditches and herding swine, filling their bellies with husks as the Party and the Army turns right? Will they be allowed to come home, repent, or will they now be branded counter-revolutionaries?"

For it is a peculiarity of Marxist theory that a counter-revolution can come just as easily from the left as the right: he was not surprised when he read that Kuai Ta-fu, the most radical of the Red Guards, had been arrested and charged with "bourgeois anarchism."

"Whatever that is…"

But all of this was academic: no-one was listening to Ed anyway, he and Lois in voluntary exile in Geneva, Switzerland, where they bought and renovated an old farmhouse and he sat in a rocking chair under a bare tree and began to think about death, the other side of the river.

It was a sick, weary, but resolutely undaunted Ed who arrived in Peking in July, 1970. Red Star was still not available in the bookshops, but he excused them: it contained too many positive portraits of too many people who had been purged in the last few years. But he was greeted as a "friend," taken on the inevitable grueling round of visits to model factories, model communes and interminable sessions of MaoZeDong-Thought:

"It's like a religious service," he complained to Lois: "How many times must it be repeated? What am I doing here," he fretted: "wasting my time, and I have so little left."

They took him back to Yenan and Pao-an, where he saw his famous picture of Mao in his cap adorning the old cave. Under the spell of that site, Ed tried to liven things up with an impromptu limerick:

"Mao Zedong was a poet of note,

Who lived by writing things to quote."

He showed it to his Chinese hosts, who didn't think it was funny.

He met up with Rewi Alley, ageing and alone, his adopted children taken from him, one of them sent to a labor camp for re-education.

Ed said he'd do what he could, but knew as he said it that it was nothing: all around he saw signs of the crackdown on any dissent, any deviation, any criticism:

"All rival thought is heresy in the eyes of a rising new priestcraft now powerfully installed in the Party with Army support," he jotted in his diary.

Lois was with him this time: she was planning a book to be called "China on Stage." Jiang Qing had taken them to the theatre to see "The White Haired Girl." Afterwards they went backstage and Jiang Qing showed the cast how they should have performed it:

"The word 'Hate' must be shouted like a grenade being hurled at the enemy; 'Spring' should be screeched to convey its political content, and you," she turned to the actress playing the heroine: "you should bristle with class hatred. When you cry, don't sit down with your head buried in your hands: cry standing up in defiance."

In Lois' gleaming eyes, Ed saw his own erstwhile naive enthusiasm. She was a convent-girl, and was enraptured by China's squeaky-clean morality, its proclaimed selfless devotion to the cause which was, of course, no less than the creation of "socialist man: pure, dedicated, sincere - a new and nobler man."

"Woman too," added Jiang Qing, turning her face to the cameras to catch the light.

As for the Chairman, Ed found him bundled up in dressing gowns and blankets: he looked like an Egyptian mummy. He was clearly dying but Ed realized that the mummification had begun long ago. Mao was wrapped in his own myth - one Ed himself had helped wind.

But they spoke frankly, Ed asking if the personality cult, the deification was really necessary: "Why do you need this? Everyone knows you're the main author of the revolution."

Mao replied that everyone likes to be worshipped but:

"We're going to put an end to it. Not all at once though," he added: "that would give the wrong impression, as if Mao was sinking..."

Of all his titles - Great Teacher, Great Leader, Great Supreme Commander, Great Helmsman - Mao said only the simple "Teacher" title should remain:

"I'm really just a lone monk walking the world with a leaky umbrella."

It was great quote, and Ed wrote it down, even though the interpreter leaned over and whispered that a better translation of what Mao had just said would be:

"Like a monk holding an umbrella, I defy laws human and divine."

Loyal to the last - if not to the man then to his vision of him - Ed said he preferred his own translation. And when the interpreter insisted, for these were Mao's words, they had the power of life and death in them, Ed replied testily:

"You have your Chairman Mao and I have mine."

All this time, Mao was adding hot water to Ed's tea cup, indifferent to their bickering: he just spoke the words, it was up to others to work out what they meant.

And then he sat back and delivered his message, the message he wanted Ed to take back to America with him, the message Ed had been waiting and wanting to deliver all his adult life. This was not his China, and America sure as hell wasn't his America, but Ed believed in people, not governments and he loved these two peoples, one with the love of a wayward son, the other that of a parent for an adopted child. If only they could be friends...

Chou En-lai had hinted at it already. Chou too was sick, ageing, his hand shook as he offered Ed sugar for his coffee, but he wanted to take Ed to see something, he said. It turned out to be a ping-pong match between China and North Korea and at first Ed had not understood - "it was too inscrutable for my Occidental mind" - even when Chou said something about even enemies being able to play sport together.

But now Mao was spelling it out for him:

"You know, if Nixon wants to come to Peking, you may bring him a message. He can come secretly if he prefers or just get on a plane and come."

Ed was stunned: Nixon, McCarthy's sidekick, the man who had three times threatened China with nuclear weapons, the man the Chinese press called "The God of Plague and War"!?

"He's a good fellow," said Mao grinning: "I like reactionaries: they help the world revolutionary cause more than wishy-washy liberals. What would we have done without Japan, without Chiang Kai-shek? You tell Nixon I think he's a good fellow, the number one good fellow in the world. But tell him not to wait too long: I'm getting old, I'm not that well. Soon I'm going to heaven."

He was sitting outside, by the pool, in a rattan rocking chair, as the sun went down:

"Sometimes," he said, "I feel like just jumping in and floating away - over there, past Coal Hill, Deng's house, the Summer Palace - all the way to the Western Paradise: that's what my mother used to call Heaven. Other times, I sit and wait for someone to come in the other way, a figure of ice, on skates, who'll reach out, take my hand..."

He shivered:

"Sunset is very beautiful, but dusk is approaching. It's nearly time for me to report to Marx."

ɟlɒw Tɦɛ Swɑllɒw Lɒst Its Tɑil: Pɑrt Tɦrɛɛ

One day Lao Kou came to the village and said the government had decided China needed more English teachers. Foreign friends would soon be invited back and he had put my name on the list: it would mean two years in Peking.

I didn't want to go: I hadn't chosen to live and work in Nanjie village, but I had come to love it, nestling in the folds of the green hills. In the evenings the light was soft velvet - we say like dove feathers. When I left, I took a pot of wild flowers up to Peking with me and put them on the window sill of my little room where they could watch the swallows fly South.

At Peking University, they gave me a dictionary and told me to memorize three pages of words a day. I learned to read and write but I have not learned to speak the language well: there was no-one to teach us proper pronunciation.

Lao Kou was angry when I refused to move into a new two-room apartment with him, preferring to stay in the student dormitory, but I no longer listened to him. In China, success at school has always been the way to shine and climb: all around me I saw people, including the new, the young people - the children of cadres and leaders - whose only concerns were their career, their grades, a good job, possessions.

But then, in May 1966, a poster went up, attacking the author of a play which had suggested that Chairman Mao was a corrupt Emperor who should be removed from office.

At first I took no notice: I have never been interested in the theatre, but then Jiang Qing came to the campus.

I admired Jiang Qing. People called her the White-Boned Demon and the Dowager Empress, said she had ambitions to succeed Chairman Mao, but I think the real problem was that she was a woman who dared speak her mind. I had met her before - in Yenan and later, when she came on an inspection visit to Nanjie and criticized Lao Kou for having a man not a woman lead the discussion:

"In the sphere of production," she said: "women are fundamental. Labor is the basic force of production, and all labor is born of women."

When the peasants hissed, she yelled at them:

"Man's contribution to human history is nothing more than a drop of sperm!"

And now, at Peking University, she got up on the stage:

"Chairman Mao sends you his greetings," she began and, when the thunderous applause had died down: "I am Chairman Mao's secretary: anything that is in his hands is also in my hands. He has placed me in charge of reforming the Chinese stage. History is made by the people, yet the old opera presents the people as though they were dirt, and the stage is dominated by lords and ladies and their pampered sons and daughters. They are paving the way for the restoration of capitalism - and not only on the stage. The same lords and ladies have taken over the stage of real life too."

It was their cue: the next day they dragged Wang Guangmei, the wife of President Liu Shao-chi, on the stage. They had lured her to the campus by getting her daughter to phone her and say she'd had a terrible car accident. They cornered her at the hospital gate and dressed her up in a silk gown, high-heeled shoes, a wide brimmed straw hat and a necklace of gilded ping-pong balls with skulls painted on them.

Wang Guangmei was no peasant: Guangmei means "Beautiful

Daughter of a Glorious Household," but "Mei Guo" is Chinese for America, where her father had worked for the Republican government. She had a degree in nuclear physics, spoke many foreign languages, dressed in foreign clothes. American spy, overqualified graduate, friend of foreigners: she was everything that was bad, but when they began to torture her, I left.

Out in the streets, Peking seethed: everywhere Red Guard battalions paraded with gongs and cymbals and drums, holding giant pictures of Chairman Mao. They were ecstatic:

"Chairman Mao is the red, red, red sun in our hearts," they sang.

"We are going to take over the country," they cried out: "wrest it back from the traitors and backsliders, return it to Chairman Mao."

They were a shock, these children, though I understood how they felt. For ten, fifteen years they had been fed a diet of stirring ideas and then walked out and saw the timid betrayals and normal compromises of their parents. It gave them that puzzled look which adults say shows they are growing up at last. But the children ascribed it all to guilt and weakness and cowardice, having no idea how ideas recede the more you try to catch them, lucky if you can still glimpse them occasionally on the far, red horizon when resting from turning the soil. But now Chairman Mao had told them to rise up and root out the four olds: China was going to be dragged in dunce caps and red armbands, shouting and weeping, out of three thousand years of passive withdrawal and cheerful hypocrisy by means of the sheer enthusiasm, ruthless dogmatism and joyful irreverence of children.

As I wandered the streets, I saw them ransacking the museums, stripping the theatres of their costumes of mandarins and emperors and concubines. They emptied bookshops of their contents and burned the books in the gutter, raided hardware shops for axe handles and iron pipes. In the parks, they pulled up all the flowers and dragged out couples they found making love in the bushes and chased them away, bare bottoms waggling like moons surprised by the sun. Cats they hanged from trees. Women were stopped in the street and given a Yin-Yang haircut: one side shaved bare, the other left untouched.

Then they took a raft out on the lake, rocking and singing, laughing and carefree under the blank blue sky, chanting: "If you are not completely reborn, you can never enter the door of Communism."

Someone was organizing them - their transport, their shelter, their food: I took the opportunity to get out of the city, go back to Nanjie. The trains were free: you could go anywhere if you wore a red armband. But in Nanjie, I found that a Red Guard battalion had preceded me: they had burned down the pagoda and smashed the ancestral tablets the peasants kept in their houses. Lao Kou gave them a welcoming banquet with lots of wine and a big pail of water with ginger in it to stop them catching colds. When they tried to put up posters denouncing him, they found he'd already covered the walls with quotations from Chairman Mao. They called a meeting and denounced him for "Waving the red flag to oppose the red flag," accused him of being a Confucian. When he protested, they yelled at him:

"Confucius is not just an ancient sage who wrote books two thousand years ago. Confucius is anyone who tells people they must obey without asking them if they agree; Confucius is anyone who says that a decision has been made and not how it has been made."

Then they turned to the peasants:

"And you," they yelled: "you are Confucians, all of you. A Confucian is not just someone who oppresses his wife and tells his children to study and become powerful. No: a Confucian is anyone who does not have an opinion, anyone who obeys an order without knowing the reason for the order, anyone who lets a mistake go by without criticizing it."

The peasants asked what they should do, but the Red Guards said:

"Dare to think, dare to speak, dare to act. You should not take orders any more from anybody."

The peasants looked at each other; Lao Kou got up and said:

"We must thank the little red general for bringing us Chairman Mao's new instructions."

"They are not instructions!"

"But Chairman Mao is our leader."

"There are no leaders!"

They relieved him of his duties, told the peasants their private plots were confiscated, but the peasants said they could not work the communal land without a cadre to tell them what to do. The children told them they should spend the time writing confessions but they said: "we cannot write, little general, and our minds are too old to learn."

When the children ordered them to do it, they said: "But didn't you say we were not to take orders from anyone any more?"

When I arrived, I found the bamboo and maize-leaf fences round the private plots had been burned down, the mud walls of the pigsties smashed, pigs and ducks and chickens scratching at the communal fields. There was no seed and Lao Kou was under guard in the school latrine.

He had lost two teeth, his lip was cut, one eye puffy, his spectacles broken:

"Will you give me that little ceramic vial I know you have? I don't think I can take any more humiliation... They say I must make a full confession," he went on, "but what they really want is for me to denounce Chu Teh. I told them I know nothing, but that you, perhaps...?"

So it was that I found myself standing on a table in the communal canteen being interrogated:

"In Pao-an, you delivered messages between Chu Teh and Chairman Mao?"

"Yes."

"What did they say?"

"I don't know, I never read them."

"You must have been tempted...?"

"No."

"Didn't Chu Teh once send you to Chairman Mao with a letter written with poisoned ink?"

"No, never..."

"How do you know that if you never opened them? Isn't it true that he tried to make you a camp whore?"

"No!"

"But you did sleep in his bed. Didn't you?"

"No. Yes, but..."

"There was an American journalist there and he did try to rape you, didn't he?"

Where had they got this information?

I soon found out: they brought in a girl, dressed like them in a khaki uniform and cap but when she looked up, I saw it was my daughter.

"Do you still deny the charges?"

"Yes."

"She gave the American journalist notes," said my daughter: "then she aborted their child and left it for the dogs."

"Give her the aeroplane!" they called out then.

"She sabotaged the Great Leap Forward by keeping back her own property from the furnace," said my daughter: "Search her and you'll find it: a dagger with a bone handle."

"Shave her head with it," they cried out then.

But I said:

"You are too late."

I took the dagger out from my belt at the back, held it up:

"See: she admits it!" they cried.

"Yes, I said: "I kept this dagger back from the furnace. And you know why? I will tell you. Yes, I was raped, but not in Yenan: I was raped by Chiang's thugs."

"She should have died rather than submit," they cried.

"Then they cut off my hair and threw me in the street. This dagger I took from a landlord and, yes, I kept it and you know why? Because I knew the job was not yet over. I took his dagger, because what he stood for: that is not dead yet. It is a long way from being dead and will not die until what he stood for, what they all stood for is finally cut out like a cancer. Until then the revolution has failed - no: worse: it has not even happened!"

They didn't believe me: they were used to their victims appearing to be on their side but really bending in the wind: they cried out:

"Give her the aeroplane!"

"That too has already been done," I replied, "and by people who know a lot more about how to hurt a body than you do."

They closed in on me, but then an older man got up and stepped forward.

I say "old" but he was no more than twenty-three, twenty-four; the others made way for him; he stood and looked up at me, then said:

"She is one of us, let her down."

He asked me if I wanted to join them and I said: "Yes. You are very young but essentially you are right. We can never sail to the new world with the corpse of the old rotting in our cargo."

Kuai Ta-fu - for that was the student's name - told me I should return to Peking with them, that it would be in the streets of the capital that the battle would be won or lost. I didn't agree:

"It will be won or lost not in Peking but here, and not in the streets, but in the hearts and minds of every peasant, every bureaucrat, every cadre."

He just shook his head:

"What people have in their hearts and minds we can never know for sure."

"Yes," I said: "it will take time…"

"We do not have time. We must abolish it all: government itself must be abolished. We must destroy Peking completely, leave it to the dust and the wind, give power back to the masses. China must become a federation of independent communes."

"But…"

"Better a too-hot chilli dish than one with no taste at all."

"Chairman Mao…?"

"Better one hour of passion than a lifetime of stale kisses."

A few days later, he left with his regiment of "iron rods." He called it the Chingkanshan Regiment and I know that they went to

Peking, seized the University, turned it into an armed camp protected by barbed wire linked to high-voltage cables. All this I learned when he appeared one day in 1967 back at Nanjie Commune.

He sat down, asked for a glass of water, drank it, wiped his lips, spat on the floor:

"We pulled them all out - the President, the mayor, the Chief of Staff, made them all pass the gate. They thought they could just confess, promise to reform and then we'd put them back in power, but we told them: no-one is ever again to have power over anyone else. They said that was anarchy and when I said 'Who cares what colour the cat is?' they asked: 'But how will a federation of communes ever defend China against all the foreign powers just waiting for an opportunity to return?'

I had no answer to that."

He stopped, wiped the dirt and sweat off his thin, pointed face, smiled wryly:

"You once said to me that you became a Communist when you realized that if you were ever going to be able to live your own life properly, then the whole of China had to be changed first. Well, the task is even bigger than that. China can only be free when the whole world is free. China can only live peacefully on its communes when the whole world is made up of communes. And that is not going to happen for a long time."

"Then it's over?"

"No..."

"Then...?"

"Sleep on a wooden plank," he said: "Eat little, gather strength for ten years, review the bitter lessons for ten years.

China will soon take the Capitalist road.

It is inevitable and even correct Marxism.

I don't know how long that will last, but, one day, we will be back...."

The first of the interrogation sessions took place in mid-December.

They always started off friendly enough: tea, cigarettes, polite enquiries about our health. Then the business part began. I'd already noticed the neat stack of files on the table in front of Old Luo: he opened the first one and said:

"On October 10th, Da Wei Bo-shi said that the Chinese government tells lies."

"What?"

"Then he tried to buy train tickets, knowing it was illegal. On October 23rd, he engaged in clandestine black-market transactions in Tienjin."

"But..."

"On November 5th, he said that there were Russian secret agents in the Institute."

It wasn't just the distortions; everything anyone had said to me or I to them had been written down the same day and handed in the next morning.

I wondered which was Yen Wei's file: probably the really fat one.

And at first I do try to explain what I'd meant when I'd said or done those things. They listen, make notes, but it soon becomes clear that the only thing at issue here is when I am going to admit I am wrong.

I'm not sure what happens if I do... And really I am too tired: yes, I've been a fool but, as Yin Wei says, that's their problem, isn't it?

"All I asked for is a reason..."

"The Chinese government does not have to give explanations to foreigners."

"No, but if you believe in a system, shouldn't you challenge it to work properly, or should you stand by and watch it betray itself?"

"He is not a citizen of China."

"So?"

"He cannot say whether decisions are correct or not."

"Can you?"

"Of course: the correct decisions are passed on to us by our leaders after all the facts have been analyzed."

"But sometimes your leaders may be wrong."

"He must not speak like this."

"Chairman Mao told us to dare to speak, dare to criticize, dare to rebel."

"He must submit to the dictatorship of the proletariat."

"What proletariat? Are those the hands of a worker? Sometimes I think Confucius is not dead: he's simply joined the party."

"He has just insulted the Chinese Communist Party."

I open my Little Red Book, read out aloud to them what it says there:

"In our country bourgeois ideology will continue to exist for a long time. All erroneous ideas, all poisonous weeds, all ghosts and monsters must be subjected to criticism."

I look up: "I think..."

"It does not matter what he thinks: we cannot know what people think: this is subjectivism..."

"Where the broom does not reach, the dust will not vanish of itself."

"Left-wing opportunism."

"After the enemies with guns have been wiped out, there will still be enemies without guns."

"Anarchism."

So much for the Little Red Book: I put it away, feeling slightly foolish, waving it around like that. It didn't even disturb the bulldust:

"If anarchism is believing that people are basically good," I say quietly: "if anarchism means that people do not need governments to tell them how to behave, if anarchism is believing that the state will one day wither away, then yes, all right: I am an anarchist. And the Cultural Revolution was anarchist and Chairman Mao is an anarchist."

There was a long silence; then:

"Da Wei Bo-shi has waved the red flag to oppose the red flag. We have offered to help him and he has refused. Measures have been decided and will now be taken against him."

The meetings continue - every day, for ten days, five hours at a time. The provocation escalates:

"The Chinese government has spent a lot of money on him and his family: on his extravagant apartment, a private cooker for his private dinner parties, special schooling for his child..."

"I did not ask for any of that..."

"He has tried to give subversive books to the Chinese teachers."

"Some of them are not on sale in China - because of censorship."

"There is no censorship: he must not say that."

"What about letters - all our letters are opened."

"Letters are not opened, unless they contain things harmful to China's culture, politics, economy, morals or hygiene."

"How do you know which letters contain such things?"

"Letters containing such things are opened."

I decide that the best thing to do is to keep silent, keep them to myself, what the Chinese call our "mouse-thoughts" - just as they call swallowing down resentment when suffering an affront having a "mouse belly."

But they are ahead of me, have done this before:

"Now we wish to talk to him about his daughter."

"What?"

"His daughter has insulted the children of China."

"What?!"

"She put all her old, worn-out toys and broken dolls in a box and tried to give them to the children at her kindergarten."

"They weren't her old toys; some of them were her favorites."

She had been very careful about it, sitting on the floor, frowning, surveying the circle of stuffed animals and selecting the ones she thought each of her friends would like best. She even consulted pink Teddy:

"She wanted to give her friends something. They have no toys of their own; she has a lot: she wanted to share them. She even consulted her own resident expert…"

"The children of China do not accept gifts from foreigners. He should discipline his daughter… We should never have sold her to him."

My knees are twitching, legs seething, toes wriggling: I need something to distract me, block out these taunting provocations:

"He who knows does not speak,
He who speaks does not know.
Close your windows, shut your doors,
Soften your anger, loosen your knots.
The best warrior is never aggressive.
The best fighter is never angry.
The best tactician does not engage the enemy…"

That's when I saw the matchboxes.

I'll never use a lighter again.

Chinese matches are long; if you tip all the matches out of two boxes, you have about a hundred square-sided sticks. Place two of them on a table, parallel, about an inch apart, then two more lying across them, at right angles: you have a square. Now add two more and, if you concentrate really hard, you can build a very pretty and quite tall pagoda. You have to concentrate especially hard as you reach the top or it will all fall down.

I'm not proud of it, but it did enable me to keep control of myself. One of the saddest, most frustrating experiences we all have to go through is discovering that the opinions people have of you are not really about you at all, but about themselves, that their opinions of you are vital to their opinion of themselves.

They have to see me as a selfish, bourgeois pig or wild-eyed anarchist or else none of it makes any sense any more.

And we'll all have to build new pagodas to new gods.

After five hours they stop:

"He may go now."

I get up.

"We hope he is still a friend of China?"

"Of the people, yes: they have great courage."

Outside, the car was late and I waited in the cold, dark, starless night. I wandered down to the commune but it was deserted, only a bony horse waiting patiently in the shafts of an empty cart, its mane plaited with red wool like an ancient tart putting on revolutionary airs.

Tracey joins me there:

"Why do the leaves turn red in autumn?"

"Oh, I expect someone gives an order: everyone turn red. Then they all fall off. No, sorry - it's a joke..."

Not very funny, Daddy.

We're in a hole: we have no passports, no visas, are unable to import money, unable to buy a ticket - to anywhere. Either I go back to work - and Bei Dai He and all - or my wife and children will be deported and I will stay - until I crave an ice-cream on the beach.

No: they're wrong. Aren't they? The right to strike is granted by the Chinese constitution: I looked it up. But I also read the decision of the State Council dated August 3rd 1957: "Anyone not working, or out of work, or who refuses a work assignment is to be arrested and confined without trial in a labor camp for an indefinite period of time."

I don't know if it's still valid: I don't think I want to find out.

A week later, Yen Wei is waiting for me at the bridge.

She says: "I am going away soon. They are saying you are a black element."

"Can't you tell them...?"

"And they say they can never know what we really say to each other."

"Then it's my fault that you...?"

"It's all right," she says: "They will send me to the countryside where they can keep an eye on me. They already have a file on me - and on my daughter... Here:"

She holds out her exercise book:

"I have made a few changes..."

"Then...?" I ask: "It's not just a story? You...?"

"It is a story," she says: "But that does not mean it didn't happen."

205

IV

THE PRODIGAL SON

Ed delivered Mao's message: Kissinger was delighted with its Machiavellian overtones: ping-pong diplomacy was right up his alley:

"So, they want to come back in from the cold, do they? Want to do business: good. Can you imagine a market of a billion consumers? When the Prodigal Son wants to return home, the least we can do is meet him half-way."

Ed wasn't there when Nixon flew in on Air Force One - "The Spirit of '76" as it was called. The final irony is that he who had desired nothing more than that China and America should be friends, died three days before Nixon bounded down the steps and shook Mao's hand.

His insides had been eaten away from all those years in China. They tried operating, but the cancer in his pancreas had already spread to the liver. At the last moment a medical team flew into Geneva from China: George Hatem, who had crossed over with Ed into Pao-An thirty-six years ago, had been sent to see if Chinese medicine could help. It couldn't. But they could chat about the old days, and the Chinese herbs did give him as comfortable and dignified an end as was medically possible.

When they stripped his body for cremation, they found an elastic band on his wrist. They were going to pull it off, but Hatem said:

"Leave it on. It probably meant something to him."

He died peacefully in the early morning of February 15th, the first day of the Chinese lunar New Year.

He left a will in which he asked that his ashes be scattered over the city of Peking: "and say that I loved China. I should like part of me to stay there after death as it always did during life."

An urn with some of his ashes was flown over and buried in a quiet spot in Yenching University. A student read a passage Ed had written when he first left:

"Part of me will always remain with China's tawny hills, her terraced emerald fields, her island temples seen in the early morning mist, a few of her sons and daughters who had trusted or loved me. I was proud to have known them, to have straggled across a continent with them, to have wept with them, her brown, ragged, shining-eyed children, the equals and lovers I had known..."

How The Swallow Lost Its Tail: Part Four

In 1975, a man came to my room. He said his name was Tang, and that he was a friend of my daughter. I noticed that his fingers had been frost-bitten: black, twisted. I could not let him stay, but he said that was all right; all he wanted from me was rice coupons. I said, yes, all right, but then he said:

"And a pair of ice skates."

I said he could hire ice skates at the Summer Palace, but two days later he came back and said there is no way in from the Summer Palace, that they've put up a new barbed wire fence, but he still needs the skates. And a long knife:

"There is a way in from Madame Soong's palace," he said, his hands shaking, forehead dotted with drops of fever-sweat: "Then under Silver Ingot Bridge, past Deng's house, the Defense Building, Coal Hill... I can pretend I'm an ice-cutter..."

Then he stopped: he had been babbling out loud and was now fearful he had already let too many mice out. I asked him how he knew my daughter?

"She was Kuai's mistress, his concubine. It was her idea: she said she knew how to get into Chongnanhai. You know she was one of the Chairman's 'long-life virgins,' don't you? If anyone could get close enough to him, they could."

But in 1966 at the height of the Cultural Revolution, the Chairman had suddenly changed residence. His new place was well guarded, but there was a swimming pool - overlooking Central Lake. It was fed by a river, which runs all the way from the Summer Palace...

All this he knew already. And he knew more than that:

"Your daughter said you know about poisons?"

"What?"

"That you have a vial of poison?"

"I don't even know where it is, I haven't seen it for many years..."

"It doesn't matter," he said: "I know what I have to do. There are bamboos in the park. And caterpillars..."

He rolled a cigarette, puffed on it, and through the writhing smoke, he said:

"When did you last see him on television? Are they keeping him prisoner? Or is he senile? Did you see him meeting Nixon? He couldn't even stand by himself, they had to lift his arm just to shake hands."

He got up, paced the room like a caged squirrel:

"He can't know what's going on."

"Perhaps he does," I said softly: "Perhaps he knows. And approves?"

He grunted:

"Either way, he deserves to die well. Usefully... There is still one last task he can perform for the revolution. Either he has betrayed us too and so deserves to die, or he too has been betrayed and his death must expose those who have killed him. Then the masses will rise up again..."

I said:

"Maybe he is already dead..."

"What?"

"And they are just waiting for the right moment to announce it. It makes no difference. The Cultural Revolution was the last battle, Tang. And we lost. Lost because we got too close. But we did get close, we could have made it. We'll always have that."

He left then. He never came back. So I don't know if he ever got in. We will never hear about it in any case and, really, it doesn't matter. He's been dead for some time now. Our Emperors do not die when their bodies die; they die when their successors are ready to take over. And they are nearly ready: China, their China has decided it has had enough. Now that we are a nation again, powerful again, feared, it is time to join the rest of the world. China, their China, wants to become a country like any other. Bigger, of course, the biggest, and clever of course, the cleverest. But playing the same game as everyone else and by the same rules.

A country, not the country (have I got it right at last, those devilish articles you invented to stop us learning how you think...?)

But a country or the country, it is my country and I love my country: I love its hills, its rivers, its mountains. China, my China, is made not just of ideas but of earth, rock, water, bone. The yellow earth has replaced the red book and its lessons are simpler but just as urgent: how to hold the shaft of a hoe so it won't rub at the blisters, how to tell a weed from a rice shoot, how much grey ash warms the soil and how much burns the shoots.

How to stand up, slowly, one vertebra at a time.

Back in Nanjie, they are busy teaching the Red Guards to serve the people - not with black letters on white paper this time, but knee-deep in irrigation ditches or standing in the blank heat of midday on the threshing floor. The peasants enjoy their new role:

"When they first came here," they said: "the children: they told us they were going to change the face of the earth. It's still earth. It still shakes when there is a bad government and quakes before the Emperor dies. And you," they tell them: "you've still got two legs and two arms, and a belly, too, eh? And one day, you'll turn into earth too. We are only guests."

But now that China, my China, has decided it wants to become just another country, now that the people, my people, have decided they want what everyone else wants, it is worth remembering that we once had other dreams, other ambitions.

Where do they go in winter, the swallows?

Do you know the story about how they lost their tails? Once they had a single tail like all other birds, but when the winter came and the cold, they huddled in their caves until their tails froze to the walls of their nests. They could not move; they could only sing and they did, very beautifully. People heard them, came to catch them. To get away, they had to flap their wings very hard until they tore their body away from their frozen tail. Now they have two tails - one left, one right, so that whichever way the wind blows, they can find their way home.

When the spring comes and then fades too soon, and then summer and the earth is dry and hard, autumn and there is much thunder in heaven, they remember the winter they lost their tails and the songs they sang...

I used to think: we must not fail. China must not fail. The torch is ours and if we let it go out, it will go out for ever, for no other people is as well suited as us to carry it. Now I think you can't turn the whole world upside down just because it doesn't suit you the way it is. Of course, people fail you, let you down. They deserve pity not contempt.

They were never in Pao-an, in Yenan.

I will always be there.

It is what I shall think about when I die: then I shall be able to close my eyes...

As we fly over the Himalayas, an air hostess brings Tracey a coloring book and crayons:

"And what do you want to be when you grow up, little girl?"

"I don't know," says Tracey, opening the book at a picture of a clown in a circus:

"What do you want to be when you grow up, Daddy?"

In the end, it wasn't too hard to get out after all. The Chinese don't make gummed envelopes; they use white paste: all our letters both incoming and outgoing have been gummed down with white paste for some time now. So I wrote a letter - to the Chinese Embassy in London, who had first employed me, detailing how my contract had been broken, how we were being held virtual prisoners, against our will. I told them that The Times was pestering me for the story. David Bonavia, their Peking correspondent, had wanted to be friends before, but at first I kept him at arm's length: I didn't want them to think we were informants.

To make sure they got the message, I sat and looked up at the ceiling, picked up the phone, called David and, speaking very slowly and clearly, told him that he could come the next day and I'd give him the interview he wants - the story about me going on strike in China: "Yes, you can call it a wild-cat strike if you like. And bring a camera..."

The next morning, Dong Ming was standing at the door with an envelope.

Plane tickets to London.

For four.

"Thank you. Do you want to come in?"

He shook his head.

"How are the students getting on?"

Caroline is helping them, he says. Caroline is a Cambridge graduate with curly hair and a sharp nose: a week ago, she sent me a note, saying she'd been asked to take over my classes at the Institute, but had refused: it would be "black-legging," she said. But then they promised her a week in a commune and now she's teaching my class.

It's not really surprising that they have a pretty low opinion of us.

"And Yen Wei?" I ask.

Dong Ming said he didn't know.

Good.

She and I have said our Farewells already – up on a small hillock on the campus of Peking University, which was called Yenching University when Ed used to teach there - so long ago. It overlooks a small lake they call "No Name Lake." Ed's ashes had been brought there in an urn and buried under a small marble stele.

I didn't know whether or not to take flowers.

As I walked across the campus in the twilight, students in white gauze face-masks loomed and then faded away, ghostly in the mist. The basketball court was deserted, the posts like gallows. A few stubborn leaves still clung to the poplars, rattling like drying voices in the breeze; a small fire burned under a tree, the smoke catching a falling leaf and playing with it. Down by the lake the willows looked at themselves in the water, anxious to see if their buds have behaved. Some had opened too early and were frozen brown and brittle and will never flower.

She was already there when I arrived, a solitary sentinel in padded jacket, padded trousers, fur hat, only her two plaits sticking out defiantly.

She looked up when she saw me, then scanned the shadows:

"I am going away too. Perhaps Tibet. They say there is much work to be done up there."

"I don't think you're very popular in Tibet."

"I will speak softly: we have shouted too much already."

"Be careful they don't convert you to Buddhism. On the other hand, then you could have many lives... If you did, how would you want to come back?"

"Is this a game?" she asked: "another game you play with Tracey?"

"No: this is a game only adults play."

"If I come back..." She paused, consulting her heart: "If I came back, I'd want to be Chinese..." She gave a little shy, embarrassed smile: "I know them best. And as a woman: we have further to go, but a better chance to get there. And I'd want to come back in the same time because this has still been China's best time..."

We both looked down at Ed's grave and then she suddenly knelt, took a knife out from her belt at the back, scraped away some of the hard frozen soil until she'd made a shallow grave of her own and dropped something in it. Before she could cover it over, I saw that it was a pen.

She stood up, wiped the dagger clean on her sleeve, put it

carefully in her belt behind her back, looked down and said:

"It was empty. His story is finished. Mine too - soon. Perhaps yours also…?"

Yes - but I can go, I can leave, start again, somewhere else; I've had a dream punctured and that is painful, but this woman - and there are millions like her - for her, for them, there is no way out.

We looked at each other: in France we'd kiss on the cheek, in America we'd shake hands, but I've never found out how to say goodbye in Chinese: "Tsai jien" means "We shall meet again…"

She turned to go:

"Oh," she added, swiveling her head: "if you write about us, don't be too hard on Old Luo: he wasn't always like that, and he wasn't always called Old Luo either…" She smiled: "Lao Kou means Old Dog: not a good name to have nowadays…"

"And your daughter?"

"It's all in here," she said, handing me a brown envelope. I put it quickly inside my jacket to nestle in the sheepskin.

"And good luck, Da Wei Tong-zhi: if you are reborn, I hope the next time you don't have such round eyes. They let in too much light… You can go blind that way…"

She walked away into the night and I don't need to ask myself why I have come to love these people.

As we fly over Tibet, I look out of the window and imagine a truck climbing slowly up the twisting road to the high plateau, and a woman, in the back, wrapped up against the cold, swaying to the rhythm of the long, winding road.

There are ice caves up there where people go and sit for three years, three months, three days and meditate on Nirvana.

The girl with kaleidoscope eyes.

Now that China has become a symbol of hard-working materialism, now that ambition is back and envy, competition and privilege, it is worth remembering that it once sang a quite different song, stood for something the world had never seen before, and will never see again.

213

Strawberry Fields. For ever...

"Where's China now?" asks Tracey, looking up from her coloring book:

"Oh, over there. Yesterday..."

"Where's yesterday?"

The other side of the stars...

175325